Emerging from
Darkness Falls

By: Kira Adams
http://kristakakes.blogspot.com
https://www.facebook.com/KiraAdamsAuthor
http://www.wattpad.com/user/xKiraAdamsx
http://www.goodreads.com/author/show/7179367.Kira_Adams

© 2015 Krista Pakseresht. All Rights Reserved.

<u>Darkness Falls Series</u>
<u>Into the Darkness</u>
Emerging from Darkness

Cover designed by <u>Cover Me Designs</u>
Editing by Joanne LaRe Thompson

This book is a work of fiction. Names, characters, places, and events are the product of the author's imagination or used in a fictitious manner. Any resemblance to actual persons or events is purely coincidental. No part of this book may be reproduced or used in any manner without the written permission of the publisher, except by a reviewer who may quote brief passages for review purposes only.

One – The Bitter End

Cullen

I never thought it would all end this way.

"On your knees!" A dark-haired Degenerate screams at Ike as he forcefully throws him to the ground. Ike and his partner have also had the misfortune of having their hands tied behind their backs.

We are screwed. This is all my fault. I led them here, and now, we are all going to pay the price for it.

I look to my right, where Ike and an unfamiliar teenager are on their knees next to me. There are three Degenerates standing before us, one equipped with a rifle, and the other two with knives. The Degenerate holding the rifle looks no older than twenty one. He has shaggy brown hair and green eyes. There is a scar across his eyebrow and I wonder how he acquired it. I'm curious how long he's been a Degenerate; how many people he has killed.

He is pointing the rifle into the face of the blond teenager who is breathing heavily and teary-eyed. I lock eyes with Ike, and it's enough to realize that this isn't the end for us. *It can't be*. We've come too far to die now.

Without being too obvious, I lean back. Enough to touch my hands to the ground. I am touching the dirt with my fingers, trying to find anything I can use to cut my ties. I find what feels like a sharp, jagged rock and begin carefully running my binds across it. The other Degenerates are too focused on their leader with the gun to notice what I am up to. I have to take advantage of this.

The young Degenerate shoves his rifle into the face of the blond teenager making him quiver with fear. He is begging, pleading for his life. He is telling them he will do whatever they want if they just let him live, and they are laughing like the sadistic bastards they are.

"Did you just fucking piss yourself?" The one with the rifle asks, glancing back at his minions. They begin cackling in unison. I watch as he takes the rifle and points it right at the crotch of the teenager's pants. "Holy fucking shit, he pissed himself."

It's almost too much for me to watch. I turn my focus back on freeing myself from the restraints.

"Please! Please!" he cries.

"You don't have to do this," Ike says calmly, turning the attention on himself.

"Oh no?" the Degenerate asks in a condescending tone. "And what…you just expect us to let you go? To let you live? Hell no, you'd kill us the first chance you got."

Ike shakes his head. "None of this has to end in bloodshed. We have a good thing going here. You guys could join us. We are going to begin rebuilding."

The Degenerate laughs, looking back at the others behind him. "And what? We'd all live happily ever after and sing Kumbaya? Yeah, right." He snorts and then turns the gun back on the blond. "No, we have orders and we intend to follow them through."

Everything happens in slow motion then. My hearing intensifies as I hear him pull the trigger, and the bullet dislodge from the gun. I still have no idea who this teenager is, but the idea that he is going to die for being in association with us, eats me up inside. The bullet meets his flesh, and his body falls roughly to the ground.

"Shit! It went straight through him! Did you see that, guys?" the gunman brags, as he steps closer to the body to get a better look.

He shot him in the head. *Poor guy didn't even stand a chance.* I can hear my heartbeat pounding in my ears as I fight with the ropes around my wrists. I know the rock is making headway into the ties, but not fast enough. I hear the footsteps inching closer as I glance up. The gunman is now in front of Ike.

Ike turns his head to lock eyes with me. I want to say something, but I can't with the duct tape across my lips. Ike smiles weakly. "They won't win," he says softly.

"I guess that's where you're wrong," the gunman states calmly, pointing the rifle in Ike's face. "Degenerates always win."

When he pulls the trigger, I close my eyes because I can't see my friend go out like this; in cold blood. But something happens that has me opening them like blinds. The gun jams. It's only a second, but enough time for Ike to make a move. I watch as Ike plows into the gunman, throwing the rifle to the ground. Ike is a hell of a fighter, even when he is tied up.

I feel the last bit of my rope break on my wrist ties, and I charge one of the other Degenerates with as much force and speed as I can muster. I knock the knife out of his hands, and wrap my hands around his neck, gripping until I feel the life go out of his body. I'm not sure if he's dead at this point, but I'm not waiting to find out. I reach for the knife from the ground, hastily cutting all the ropes that bind me.

I feel a sharp pain in my side and look up to find the last Degenerate standing before me, his knife drawn and dark, red blood spilling from the tip of it. I stagger backwards, falling to the ground. The Degenerate raises the knife in the air as if he is about to stab me again, when I hear the deafening sound of a gunshot. The Degenerate falls on top of me, lifeless.

I feel the pressure lighten as I see Ike, now free, pulling the dead Degenerate off of me. As he helps me to my feet, I notice the Degenerate I choked earlier begin moving. Ike rips the tape off of my mouth. "What are we going to do with him?" I motion with my head, knowing our time is running out.

Ike glances away from me and at one of the bases of the treehouses. "We are going to get some answers."

We use the same ropes that had previously held us captive to tie him up, hanging him upside down from one of the lower branches. He is hissing and squirming, tossing threats our way left and right.

"Where did they take them?" Ike asks, pressing

one of the knives to his throat.

Instead of answering, he spits directly into his face. Ike wipes it off and then ends up cutting both his wrists. The Degenerate screams from pain, breathing in deeply. I glance around, already feeling the dragging feet in our direction.

"I guess you'll just have to bleed out then," Ike bites under his breath. We begin to walk away when the Degenerate finally gives in.

"Wait! Wait!" he screams. "Don't leave me here. I'll tell you where they took them! I'll tell you everything!"

Ike leans in so that he is closer to the traitor's mouth. "Talk."

I am gripping my side from the pain and to keep pressure on my wound, but I can tell I am losing a lot of blood. I am swaying from side to side, weakly. "Ike," I call out to my friend.

He holds up his hand as he continues listening to what the enemy has to say.

I stumble over to one of the other tree bases and lean against it. I can barely keep my head up. I can see the biters in the distance, making their way slowly toward us. "Ike, we have to move!" I say with more urgency.

He lifts his head and follows my gaze. I watch as he pulls on the ropes, lifting the Degenerate even further up into the air. He is dangling upside down about ten feet off the ground. "I thought we had a deal!" he cries.

Ike double knots the rope before looking back at him. "A Degenerates' word means nothing. You are now our escape plan."

He rushes over to me, toting the rifle, and then throws his head under my arm and quickly maneuvers us to the ladder of the treehouse. "What are you doing?" I ask.

Ike turns his head toward the road and then back to me. "We don't have time. We have to get up there, to safety."

I don't bother asking for any more explanations as we slowly make our way up the base of the tree and onto the deck of the first treehouse. We are high enough when the first biters appear, they don't even notice us. They head straight to the upside down Degenerate. He is obviously weak from his blood loss, but he is screaming, exerting the rest of his energy. Ike pulls me into the first treehouse, locking the door behind us. He drops me onto the bed and rushes around grabbing supplies to help.

The screaming seems to go on forever outside as I imagine the biter population grows below us. I blink my eyes a few times, trying to stay conscious, but soon, I've lost all the fight in me. "Stay with me, Cullen," I hear Ike faintly before my eyes roll into the back of my head and I give in to my fatigue.

Two – A Necessary Distraction

Cullen

I'm awoken by a loud bang. An explosion of sorts. As my eyes adjust, I realize I am still inside our hideout, high up in the trees. My side hurts with every intake of breath, but as I look down, it appears as though Ike has bandaged me up as well as he possibly could. My eyes scan the inside of the treehouse, but he is nowhere in sight. I can feel my heart begin to beat faster as I slowly lift myself to my feet and shakily head to the door.

Smoke is billowing in the distance, and I know it is coming from the main road. I cast my eyes downward toward the hanging Degenerate. Besides a couple of stragglers, most of the biters have begun making their way toward the smoke. The Degenerate is not moving anymore, and it's clear he is dead. I make my way back inside and slip my shirt back on along with my hoodie, being very careful and precise with my movements.

When I make it back outside, Ike is climbing the ladder to meet me. "What the hell happened out there?" I ask, motioning with my head toward the main road.

"We needed a distraction to pull the biters away from here, so I created one," Ike answers simply, eyeing me down. "How are you feeling?"

I shrug. "I feel like I was stabbed."

He nods stiffly. "We are going to need to lay low for a couple of days so you can heal. But soon, we are going to need to find a new hideout."

I shake my head dismissively. "No. Phoenix and Rian are still out there."

"If there's one thing I've learned, it's that Phoenix can take care of herself," Ike replies. "We will find them, but you're going to need your strength first."

"We don't even know where they took them," I mutter, defeated.

"You're right. But they aren't shy and they aren't afraid. They are going to show their faces sooner or later and when they do...we are going to kill them," Ike says matter-of-factly.

Ike advises me to get more rest, which pisses me off to no end, but I oblige. He says he is going to find us some food. I haven't eaten in close to two days. If it weren't for the obnoxiously loud sounds my stomach is making, I wouldn't have even remembered. Too much has happened.

Ike returns shortly after, carrying a couple of cans of food. I can't sleep any longer. Not with the notion that Phoenix is out there. I know if it were me out there, she would never stop looking. The guilt is eating me away.

Ike secures the door behind him before heading straight for the two-person table. I follow him silently, attempting to get a better look of what he brought. "So we've got kidney beans and corn. Take your pick." I grab the corn and pop the lid off before walking it to the small sink and draining the water. He opens his own can and dips his fingers in, scooping the red beans into his mouth.

"Where did you find these?" I ask.

He looks at me through tired eyes. "A house a few miles out. It was bare besides these. It looked like it had already been hit."

I nod as I begin shoveling the sweet corn into my mouth.

As we continue to eat in silence, I look over at my longtime friend. He looks worn down and tired with bags under his eyes. His wrinkles are more noticeable and I wonder if the overall chaos has aged him. "You know, I never got a chance to say I'm sorry about what happened to Robyn and Asia."

Ike immediately stops eating and locks eyes with me. I can tell I've struck a nerve. He swallows a few times before beginning to blink rapidly. He sets the half-eaten can of kidney beans on the table and stands. He is out the door moments later.

I know losing his family wasn't easy on him, but we've never spoken about it. It's just never been the right time. I remember our countless deployments overseas where Asia and Robyn were the only things that kept him going; the only reason he held onto hope. I don't know how he's been able to hold it together so well, but I envy him. I barely know Phoenix and being away from her has been like torture. The fact that she may never know how I feel about her, kills me inside.

I finish off my can of food and then make my way outside. The moon is illuminating the dark sky and there is a slight breeze. Although it's nearing November, the nights in Tennessee aren't too cold. Ike is leaning over the railing of the rope bridge, his head held down. I hesitantly make my way toward him, and it's the first time I've ever seen him cry. I'm not sure how to act, what to do. I feel guilty for bringing up such a grim subject.

"Look, I'm sorry man, I didn't mean to..."

He cuts me off before I can finish.

"It was all my fault." His voice is shaky and staggering. "I'm the reason they're dead."

I inch closer, my voice low. "You're being too hard on yourself."

"Am I?" he asks, turning his face toward mine. "I knew my wife was infected. I just didn't want to believe it. I went to bed next to her like any other normal night. We saw firsthand what that virus did, and I just looked the other way. I should be dead. I didn't protect Asia. I was a coward."

His words shock me. I've always looked up to Ike. I've never heard him sound so weak, so defeated. I open my mouth to speak, but close it when I realize he's not finished.

"When I woke up and she wasn't in the bed...I knew. And then I found my daughter bleeding out in the living room thanks to my wife. Do you want to know the first thought that ran through my head? Relief. I was *relieved* that they wouldn't have to know the horrors that I knew were to come. I was *relieved* I wouldn't have to protect anyone but myself. Can you believe that? What kind of a sick bastard does that make me?" His voice is rising, but we are so high up, I don't stress too much about it. It's obvious he's needed to get this off his chest for a while.

"It makes you human, Ike." I sigh, breathing in the clean air. "They knew you loved them."

"A father is supposed to go to the ends of the earth to protect his family, his kids. I practically killed them myself." He is distraught with tears trailing down his face.

My heart hurts for him. I never knew how it all went down. I think part of me didn't want to know. Ike has always been the levelheaded one out of the two of us. Finding out that he isn't as strong as I thought he was, has always been a fear of mine. I reach out my hand to his shoulder and give it a reassuring squeeze. "I can't imagine the pain you feel, but I want you to know that I am here for you. I'll always be here for you."

Ike nods stiffly, sniffling.

I can only hope his family has found peace. It's the least of what they deserve.

Three – The Sick & Twisted Truth

Phoenix

My eyes flutter open and my ears begin to make out the sounds around me. I can hear bustling about, and it appears I am not alone.

I look down quickly, realizing I am tied down and currently there is an IV hooked up, draining my blood. I can barely keep my eyes open as I feel the blood exiting my system.

"What is this?" I ask weakly, to no one in particular.

I hear feet shuffling toward me, and then a French accent. "I'm sorry, my dear, they left me no choice."

"Why?" I gasp out, worried they plan to drain me.

"They will kill me if I don't manufacture the cure for them," he replies in a low voice. I recognize him. He's the doctor that Cullen found.

"Where's Rian?" I ask.

"She's safe...for now. You're the first round of testing." At least she is somewhat safe.

"Where are we?" I ask weakly.

"An abandoned hospital."

Jerrica walks in, knife raised. She has blood smeared across her clothing and my heart rate spikes. *God, please don't let that be Rian's blood.* "That's enough questions."

All I want to do is rip her throat out and tear that stupid smirk right off her face, but I can't move an inch. I'm the weakest I've ever felt.

"Why are you doing this?" I question. "We were good to you. We took you in as one of our own."

Jerrica laughs heartily. "I have my own family. I never needed yours. Just your supplies—and coincidentally, you turned into one of those supplies I needed. It's nothing personal."

"You won't get away with this." I'm fighting with everything in me to keep my eyes open, but it isn't working.

"I think I already have." Jerrica chuckles.

Cullen. Ike. Foster. The last time I saw them they

were on their knees. I want to stay positive, but I know how the Degenerates work. There's no way in hell they would have let them go without a fight. I'm sickened by the thought that we just found Cullen, only to lose him again. I'm the reason they were all in danger. I'm the reason they are probably all dead.

Even in my semi-conscious state, I hear it, a loud bang.

Jerrica motions to one of her lackeys. "Go see what that was."

I hear the door open and close.

I can still hear Jerrica's breathing. It's labored and anxious. Moments later, I hear the door bust open and Rian's familiar voice.

"How'd you get out?" Jerrica stammers. There is fear in her voice.

"I have my ways. Now let my sister go, or I'll shoot," Rian warns.

I try opening my eyes, but they are glued shut. It takes too much energy.

"Calm down, Rian," Jerrica says softly. "I thought we were closer than that?"

I hear another bang go off and a loud shriek.

"I'm done talking…"

I am dying to see with my own eyes what is happening, but I can't stay alert any longer. I surrender to the darkness.

* * *

Cullen

"Ike, it's been a week. I feel better. Can we go now?" We've been hiding out at the Treehouse Resort for longer than I would have liked. Each day making me feel guiltier than the rest. I need to find them. I need to save *her*…

"Are you sure you can make it? You were stabbed, Cullen, you're a liability."

"No! I'm tired of sitting around and doing nothing. For all we know, they've already killed them. I can't be useless any longer…not when their fate rests in our hands."

"What do you propose we do?" Ike asks.

"Kill the bastards. Every last one of them until they tell us where they took her."

"Took them," Ike corrects me.

"Yeah." I nod quickly.

A couple of days ago, when Ike was out on the hunt for food, he came across a Degenerate traveling alone. He jumped him, and we've been holding him hostage ever since. We have him tied up inside one of the other treehouses, and Ike has been working on getting him to talk. Ike has not been gentle, and I can see it in his eyes how worried he is about the girls.

I hear a scream pierce the air and I limp out the door, headed toward the noise. I look out to the ground, because of how high up we are, I'm not overly worried about attracting biters. Slowly, I make my way across the rope bridge and to the last treehouse in the resort. It's lower than ours, but still a good twenty five feet off the ground. I hear sounds of impact as I push my way inside, closing the door behind me.

The Degenerate is tied up to a chair, huddled over it, and blood is splattered all over the floor, walls, and even ceiling. He lifts his head slightly at the sound of the door, and I can now see one of his eyes is swollen shut, blood is seeping out of his mouth, and his ear is cut open.

"Cullen," Ike greets me stiffly. "What are you doing here?"

"I'm tired of waiting. Has he talked yet?" I motion with my head toward our prisoner.

"He's close," Ike replies, his jaw tense.

I shake my head, inching closer. "We're running out of time."

"Where did they take the girls?" I ask, grabbing his chin roughly in my hand.

He is middle-aged with dark eyes and short black hair. He has a goatee and tattoos cover his body. The Degenerate isn't small by any means. He is over six feet tall, and his biceps bulge out of his shirt. I'm surprised Ike has been able to contain him for so long.

The Degenerate begins cackling in a maniacal way.

"What's so funny?" I ask in a short tone. This only seems to rile him up more. He is soon gasping for breath from all of the laughing.

"You're all dead," he whispers in a deep, sinister voice.

Rage takes over my body, and I am unable to stop it. In one swift movement, I've grabbed a knife off the table and stabbed him in the leg with it. He lets out a bloodcurdling scream, the kind that gives you chills. I twist the knife back and forth, while it is still lodged deep into his leg. "Still have nothing to say?"

I can feel Ike's eyes on me. I can sense the uneasiness in the room. *He's been too polite about all of this.* I'm not willing to wait any longer. I pull out the knife quickly, and blood begins gushing out of the wound, staining the dark jeans he wears.

He is breathing deeply, and yet, the Degenerate still manages to keep a smile on his face. "You think you're so tough, but you have no idea what's coming."

I cock my head to the side. "I've been deployed three times. I've been blown out of a Humvee from an IED. I'm pretty sure I can handle whatever comes my way."

The Degenerate laughs weakly, shaking his head. He is staring at the ground, inhaling deeply.

"Alright then," I say calmly before stabbing the knife deeply into his other leg. His scream is louder this time, and I notice Ike head for the door out of the corner of my eye. He's checking to make sure we aren't going to be overridden on the ground when we finally decide to make our way out of here.

The Degenerate is cussing and hissing from the pain. He is fighting against his ties to free himself. "You have no idea who she really is, do you?" he says, barely above a whisper.

"What?" I ask, leaning down so that we are now eye-level.

He cackles in between labored breaths. "You had no idea who you *rescued* that day."

"Jerrica," Ike offers.

I glance at him questioningly, and then back to our prisoner. "What the hell are you trying to say?"

"Did she tell you about her family?" the Degenerate asks, breathing in deeply.

Ike and I exchange glances. "What about them?" I press.

"Did she tell you what she did to them? Why she ended up in prison?" I'm not sure what he is getting at, but I'm too intrigued to let it go at this point. Neither of us say anything, instead let him continue on without interruption.

"One day, when her husband was off on a run, she snuck into their rooms one by one, and she killed them."

Ike's eyes meet mine, and they are wide. I'm not sure what to believe. I swallow. "How do you know this?"

The Degenerate laughs. "The psycho bitch was bragging about it when we first picked her up. First, she started with her oldest child. He was going to be a senior in high school. She slit his throat, letting him bleed out in his own bed. But get this, she didn't stop there. She stabbed him an additional forty-eight times. Must have had some pent-up anger to release."

The way he is talking about the horrific crime makes me nauseous. I glance at Ike, knowing he was one of the closer people to Jerrica, and he doesn't seem to be taking it any easier.

"She offed her next son by suffocating him with his own pillow as he slept. She took a silencer and shot him through the pillow twelve times."

I have chills running the course of my body as the images begin making their way into my mind.

"Her next son's death was the most gruesome of them all." The way his eyes light up as he tells us about the murders intensifies the rage now spreading throughout my body.

"Shut up! Shut the hell up!" I bark into his face.

"What's wrong?" he taunts me. "You scared about what she will do to you?"

I pull the knife out of his leg so quickly, he's screaming bloody murder. I can't take any more details about her children's murders. I need to find Phoenix and Rian before she hands them the same gory fate.

"The next words out of your mouth better be the location of our people or I'm feeding you to the biters," I warn.

He begins chuckling again and I lose it. I slam the knife back down into his leg, and blood gushes out all over the ground.

He is sputtering and rambling nonsensically. There is one word that comes out of his mouth that catches my attention, *hospital*.

After he releases the exact location of the hospital, we drop the Degenerate over the side of the bridge. It is over a twenty foot fall, and he's dead by the time he hits the ground. It's enough of a distraction for us to make it down unnoticed. Saint Francis is located in Memphis, a couple of towns over. Once we find a new ride, Ike puts the pedal to the medal, and it takes less than two hours to make the commute.

After the new information we were fed about Jerrica back at the Treehouse, we are both on edge. For all we know, the Degenerate could have simply been making it all up in an attempt to rile us up, but the way he knew every sickening detail about the kills makes me uneasy. How is it possible that we were traveling amongst a serial killer with no idea whatsoever? What does that say about us?

There are biters scattered amongst the parking lot, but they don't take much notice of us. After eliminating a handful of them, we begin to make our way into the building. It is unusually quiet, and Ike keeps his rifle drawn the entire way through. I know we only have a couple of bullets left, so ideally, we will only use them as a last resort. Walking through the empty halls, the hospital appears to be in disarray. Whether it was looters or Degenerates, it appears as though a struggle took place.

I follow Ike through an open door at the end of the hall. A hospital bed, IV, and machines fill the room. There is a pool of blood near the entrance and footsteps through the blood, leading back out into the hall. My stomach drops. I lock eyes with Ike, and his expression matches mine, worry.

Something catches my attention on the far wall. Blood is smeared across it, but it looks as if it were done purposefully. I walk slowly toward the red liquid and my eyes hone in on the hand written message.

They won't win. We will be reunited.

I glance back at Ike, and he approaches to get a better look. I don't know if this is Phoenix or Rian, but for the first time in almost a week, I have hope.

Four – A Missing Connection

Phoenix

When I come to, it's obvious that we are in motion.

"Phoenix! You're awake!" I hear Rian cry.

I feel like I've been run over by a semi-truck. Surprisingly, I'm alive. "What happened?" I ask as my eyes begin to adjust, and I realize we are in an ambulance.

"Here." She hands me a juice box. "You need this. You've just lost a lot of blood."

"Where are we?" I ask, glancing around the metal box.

"We're still in Tennessee."

"Who's driving?" I ask, more alert now.

"Jean-Luc. I needed a doctor to be able to give you a blood transfusion."

I notice bandages on her arm. "You didn't…"

"I had to. You were going to die. And plus, I

have O negative blood. You needed it more than me."

"Jerrica?" I ask, assuming she'll catch my drift.

"I didn't kill her, if that's what you're asking. But I injured her enough to slow her down."

"Why not? She was going to kill you." Under normal circumstances, I would worry about tainting my young sister's mind. But she's proven she's much stronger than I even knew. She can handle the harshness of the world better than I can.

"You said it yourself. We aren't Degenerates. I want to be able to live with my choices."

I nod stiffly. "Cullen, Ike?"

"We are going back. If there's any possibility they are alive…we'll find them." Thinking about going back makes me uneasy. Especially not knowing what we are returning to.

"Are you worried about Foster?" I ask softly.

Rian shrugs, but her eyes tell a different story. "He's taken care of himself for a while now. If anyone was able to talk their way out of their predicament, it would have been him."

"Phoenix, Rian," Jean-Luc calls from the front of the ambulance. I sit up and rip the IV out of my arm. I'm still a little woozy, but thanks to Rian, I will be okay. We approach the front of the ambulance, and can now clearly see our old location. There are biters mulling about, and there are remnants of bodies lying all over the ground. Jean-Luc covers his mouth in horror, gasping.

"Stay here," I order the pair.

"But..."

"But nothing," I cut her off. "Protect Jean-Luc. I'll be right back, I promise." As I hop out of the back of the ambulance, Rian hands me a sharp knife.

"Be careful," she warns me.

"I will," I reply as she shuts the doors behind me.

The biters take notice of the noise and begin slowly making their way toward me. A biter who must have been elderly when the virus took her over reaches for me. Her wrinkled skin sags off the bone and her eyes are sunken in and bloodshot. I stab her in the head, ripping it out quickly and then fend off my next attacker. This time, it's a middle-aged man. His hair is hanging from his head, the skin dangling along with it. I kick his leg out from under him, watching him fall to the ground with a thud. I'm on top of him in the next second, my knife putting him down for good.

After taking down the majority of them, I inch toward the bodies. The stench that is wafting off the dead bodies and biters is enough to make me gag, yet far too familiar at this point. I put my arm across my face to mask the smell and lean in close, trying to get a better look. Unfortunately, the bodies are dismembered. I'm lucky to find a hand attached to an arm. There are pieces of bodies, scattered about. It's a sickening sight. I find one foot and am able to deduce that it is not any of our people. There is a Degenerate hanging from a tree, who appears to have been bled out. He is the only full body I come across.

I make my way up the ladder to our old hideout, and there are blood-soaked towels all over the floor of the first one. Tears begin to sting the back of my eyes. *Maybe they made it out? Maybe they found peace?*

I clear each and every treehouse, making sure to sweep it more than once. When it is obvious they are nowhere in sight, I leave one more message. I have no idea if they made it out of here alive, but if there is even a sliver of a chance they will return, I want them to know we are safe. I take my knife and carve out a message on the back of the door in the first treehouse.

Rian and Phoenix were here. Headed to prison.

The prisons are supposed to be a safe haven for those that survived. The Treehouse Resort is no longer safe as the Degenerates know of its location. I need to take Rian somewhere she will be safe. I'm just hoping I'm making the right decision.

* * *

Ike

"Cullen, I know you're trying to do what's right by her, but going back there? It doesn't feel right." I saw the message as clearly as Cullen did, but we still have no idea if it was Phoenix or Rian who left it. We still have no idea who it was intended for. We barely made it out of the Treehouse Resort and to head right back seems like a step backwards.

"I thought you of all people would be headlining this savior mission. Why do you seem so anxious to abandon it now?" Cullen asks me, his lips in a tight line.

He's right...but so much has transpired since we last saw the girls alive. After everything that we found out about Jerrica, I can't imagine her losing the girls, much less letting them live. For all we know, they never made it out of the hospital, and the Degenerates are simply setting up a trap for us. I know Cullen is running on pure guilt. I can see it in his eyes. He hates himself for leaving us. Now he's worried he'll never get the chance to right his wrong. I want more than anything in the world to find the girls alive, but I'm just not as convinced that they are.

"I think we need to think about this logically. There is a lot of blood here, Cullen."

"So what are you saying? You think they didn't make it?" His tone is stiff as a board.

"That's not what I am saying...but the Degenerates are still out there, and once they find out what we did to their guys, they're going to be out for blood."

Cullen sighs. I know he cares for Phoenix, as do I. Hell, I care about Rian too, but Cullen isn't even 100%.

"Let me stitch you up," I offer, opening up a few different cabinets in search of the right utensils.

He obeys.

"I want to find them alive as badly as you do," I tell him, as I begin threading the needle through his skin.

He tenses up, sucking in deep breaths from the pain.

"I just think we need to be rational about this."

"So what are you saying?" Cullen hisses.

"I'm saying that if the girls are alive, we'll find them, but in the meantime, we need to make our survival a priority."

He groans loudly from the pain.

"You trusted me before. Think you can do it again?" I ask.

He sighs. "Fine colonel. I'll let you call the shots. But if I find them and they're not living and breathing, you're on your own."

"Fair enough."

Five – Safe Among Allies

Cullen

Although I want to head back to the Treehouse Resort, I decide to trust Ike. It's nothing new to take orders from him, and he's never done me wrong in the past. He decides that what we need to do is head for the nearest prison to see if there are any survivors, food, and shelter like the reports previously stated.

Ike switches on the radio as we drive. "What are you doing?" I ask.

He glances at me and then back at the radio. "I'm trying to see how much of the world has been affected by the outbreak."

I sigh. "Isn't it obvious?" My eyes look out the windshield at our desolate surroundings.

He ignores me, instead turning the dials, attempting to find anything other than static. He stops abruptly, staring back at me. "There."

"Day 71, the virus has now traveled throughout the majority of the United States. Hawaii is still considered to be pure. Europe, South America, Africa, Asia, and the Middle

East have reported cases of the virus. No word on Australia or Antarctica yet. Casualties in upwards of hundreds of millions are being reported."

Ike and I glance at one another, uneasy. I swallow, digesting the information. The world will never be the same again.

"The government is still MIA, and I fear the worst for the remaining survivors. The world is in complete chaos. People are turning on one another, killing each other over food, shelter, and personal items. Electricity and running water are still accessible, but no one knows how long that will last. The gas stations are running out of fuel, and someday, the world will be plunged into never-ending darkness. So, this is my question for you Mr. President: where are you now? I'll tell you where you are, you're hiding like a coward while the rest of the world pays for your mistakes."

Ike turns the dial, killing the radio. Neither one of us had any idea how bad it had all gotten. Everything is doom and despair, and unfortunately, the reporter was right, it's only going to get worse. At this point, we're all doomed.

A couple of blocks outside of the hospital, we come across a gold Honda Civic LX with a forth a tank of gas. Because we're not familiar with Tennessee, we have no clue where to go. Luckily, I find a state map in the glove compartment and it directs us right to it. As we drive through the desolate cities, on our way to the prison, it is becoming more apparent what the world is coming to. Everything is lifeless, hopeless.

It takes more than an hour to locate Whiteville Correctional Facility. The streets are unusually quiet when we pull up to the gates. There are biters outside the fences, but they can't get in. We both exit the car with knives in hand, and take down a handful of biters. As soon as we aren't surrounded, I try opening the gate, but it will not budge. I hear a chorus of footsteps from inside the gates, and then I spot the military fatigues headed straight for us. There looks to be more than thirty of them, and they are all carrying rifles. None of them look even semi-friendly as they close in with straight faces.

"Who are you?" The leader of the pack asks sharply. He has salt-and-pepper hair and dark eyes.

"This is Cullen, and my name's Ike. We don't want any trouble. We heard on the news that the prisons were safe, and we were finally in a position to check it out." Ike holds up his arms in surrender, glancing at me, motioning for me to follow suit.

"How do we know you aren't infected?" a random soldier asks.

"I guess you're just going to have to trust us," I reply with a smirk. When it's obvious they have no intention of letting us in, Ike begins pulling up his sleeves and pant legs.

After he proves that he is clean, all eyes land on me to do the same. I'm frustrated, but I do it quickly as I can see biters lurking toward us, slowly.

As soon as I lift up my shirt to expose my chest, my dog tags clank against my bare skin, catching the attention of the grey-haired soldier. "Shit, why didn't you say something?" he asks in a guilty tone, already heading to unlock the gate.

"Didn't really get a chance to." I shrug.

Moments later we are allowed inside, and the fence is again secured behind us. We drive our car into the secured area, and then hear a ricochet of bullets whizzing toward where we had just been standing. I look and a pile of biters are lying on the ground, lifeless.

"I'm Pauly," the older soldier extends out his hand for me to shake. "This is Brant and Jeremiah." He motions with his head to his left and right. "We call the shots around here."

Pauly has a southern accent, while Jeremiah has what sounds like a New Jersey accent.

"How many people are here?" Ike asks, glancing around.

"Why don't you see for yourself?" Brant asks, as they lead us inside the cement walls. Eyes and faces watch our every move as we make our way through the halls.

"There has to be at least two hundred people here," I whisper more to myself than anyone else.

"Two hundred and twenty two," Pauly says surely. "Including you two and the other new arrivals."

"You had more arrivals recently?" I ask hopefully. "Any girls?"

Jeremiah nods.

"Red hair?" I press.

"You looking for someone?" Brant turns to ask

me.

"Yeah, we were traveling with two others. A redhead mid-twenties, and her younger sister."

"Well, you're welcome to take a look around. All the new recruits go into cell block C until we know they won't be a liability," Pauly states.

He leads us to cell block C, and there are at least twenty five people housed inside. It's surprising to me that all these people made their way to the prison within the last week. Every cell that I pass, heads turn and eyes fixate on mine. The pressure is rising as I near the end of the row. My eyes catch a glimpse of red hair and my heart begins to beat erratically.

Was Phoenix's hair short or long when I last saw her? I can't even think straight.

"Phoenix?" I say softly, before I can stop myself.

The girl turns around and her brown eyes lock onto mine. My heart sinks. My eyes travel over her face which is covered in freckles, and she smiles lopsidedly at me, but she is missing more than a few teeth.

"Sorry, wrong person," I stammer, turning around quickly. I end up running smack into

Ike's chest.

He looks down at me with a concerned expression. "They're not here."

I nod, pushing past him gently. "No, they aren't."

I didn't realize how badly I wanted that girl to be Phoenix. Time is no longer on our side, and the probability of Phoenix and Rian being alive is shrinking rapidly. I shouldn't have left them back at the cave. I was wrong to think I could handle it all alone; that they could handle things without me. Splitting up has only landed us in more trouble than before. I've learned my lesson. If I ever have the pleasure of staring in those sapphire eyes of hers again, I'm never going to let her out of my sight.

* * *

Ike

I can feel eyes on us as we make ourselves comfortable in the cell they set us up in. Primarily, two sets of eyes. My gaze shifts to the right and locks with a pair of stunning emerald eyes. They belong to a woman with caramel colored skin and long, curly locks. Her beauty renders me speechless for a moment.

"So, you're the fresh meat," she states.

I nod, stepping away from my cot and closer to the bars that separate us. "Ike." I reach my hand out to shake hers.

She takes my hand, shaking it delicately. "Carmen."

I look around her to the other pair of eyes. They look like a miniature version of herself. "And who might this be?" I crouch down, attempting to put myself on the little girl's level.

"That would be Neveah," Carmen says, pushing her forward. "Don't be shy."

Neveah is light skinned like her mother, and if I had to guess, around eight or nine years old. A pang in my chest deepens as I think of my own daughter.

"Cullen," I hear from behind me.

I shake my head. "I'm sorry, that's Cullen."

Carmen breaks out into a sincere smile. "Welcome to the fold."

I wave slightly before returning my attention back to my own cell.

* * *

A few hours later, I follow my rumbling stomach to the mess hall where there is more food than I have laid my eyes on in months. They serve meals when the sun comes up, when the sun goes down, and somewhere in between. Although there are clocks on the wall to tell time, they have a system and it seems to work for them.

I stand in the lunch line, and my eyes peer around at the lunchroom which is currently filled with people. It's strange to think that this is the most normal I have felt since the outbreak. It is set up buffet-style, so I help myself to a couple of bread rolls, chicken, corn, and an apple. My eyes scan the lunch room for a place to sit, when they locate the friendly female from my neighboring cell. She is seated at a table by herself with her daughter, and before I can weigh the pros and cons, I've already set my tray on the table. "Mind if I join you?"

She looks up from her tray with kind eyes. "No, go ahead."

I set my tray down on the metal table and sit down. "Hello, Neveah, how are you doing today?"

Neveah smiles shyly and then hides behind her mother.

"Neveah, don't be rude, say hi to Ike," Carmen scolds her.

"It's alright," I say gently. "My daughter is the same way." The words have already left my mouth before I process them.

"You have a daughter?" Carmen asks intrigued. "Where is she?"

I look down at my food, my appetite suddenly gone. "I wasn't thinking." I shake my head, sadly. "My daughter…she…" I trail off, unsure if I even want to explain what happened to her.

Carmen nods her head, sympathetically, her hand reaching out and landing on my arm. "I'm sorry. I didn't mean to…"

I shake my head dismissively. "It's my fault, really."

Carmen shifts her eyes to her daughter. "Why don't you go play with Max and Bianca?"

Neveah breaks into a wide grin. "Okay!"

She hops off of the bench and begins scurrying toward the opposite side of the room. I can't help chuckling.

"She's beautiful," I say softly, picking up my plastic fork.

"Thank you," she replies, locking eyes with me.

There are a few moments of awkward silence before she speaks again. "Can I ask you something?"

I nod, putting my fork down, and giving her my full attention.

"What happened to you?" She is motioning toward my arm in the sling.

I look down at it and then sigh softly. "Car accident, the car won."

She giggles. "Before or after the world went to shit?"

My eyebrow raises. "After."

She nods, pushing her empty tray away from her.

"Mind if I ask you a question now?" I take a bite of my apple.

"Sure."

"How long have you been here?" I am curious to how long they've been building this community of theirs.

She rests her elbows on the tabletop. "For a couple of weeks. We are originally from Georgia, and we were on our way to Mississippi when Brant found us."

"What was in Mississippi, if you don't mind me asking?"

She glances back at Neveah who is in a lively conversation with two other children and then back to me. "We were headed to her grandparents' house."

"But you didn't make it?" I know that I have no right to continue drilling her, but it's nice to be able to get lost in conversation.

She shakes her head, sadly. "When Brant found us they had already been through Mississippi, he said that all that was left there were biters. We had been on our own for a few weeks already, and I wanted to do whatever I could to keep her safe, so I followed them back here."

"And her father?" I know I may be pressing my luck, but I'm curious.

Carmen's eyes gloss over and I know I've upset

her.

"I'm sorry, I didn't mean to overstep."

She shakes her head dismissively. "No, it's okay. We were together when the virus began spreading. He was a police officer. His civil duty was to protect his country, and unfortunately, he died protecting it."

I swallow, setting down my half-eaten apple. "I'm sorry."

She shrugs slightly, looking down at her hands. "What about you? Were you married?"

My jaw tenses as I relive the last memories I have of my beautiful wife. I nod, silently.

Carmen senses my discomfort and decides not to push it. "I guess we've all lost people we care about."

I nod, grimly. "I keep hoping that one day I will wake up and that all of this will have been a bad dream…but it never happens."

She reaches out her hand, touching mine gently. "It's not always going to be like this. We're just being tested. It's how we react now that will mold our future."

My eyes meet hers as I digest her words. With everything she's lost, I'm surprised she has such a positive outlook. It's refreshing.

"Well, I have some chores to get done. Talk later?" She stands up from the bench, grabbing both trays in front of her.

"Chores?" I ask, curiously.

She nods, her eyes twinkling. "We all help out around here; help make things run smoothly."

I exhale silently. "I think I may like it here."

She smiles back at me. "I think you just might."

Six – Something Sinister Awaits

Phoenix

Rian swivels her head from side to side, taking in our surroundings. "So this is what a prison looks like."

I nod, warily. When the outbreak first happened, people were encouraged to make their way to the prisons. They were emptied of the Degenerates, and the rest of the civilian survivors were to find their way to the nearest jail or prison facility and take shelter behind the gates. The government was rumored to be the sole form of protection. As I too let my eyes fall upon the tall gates before us, something feels off, wrong. Not a soul is in sight. If I didn't know any better, I'd say the place is empty. What's even more disconcerting is there is no sign of biters either. I can see them walking in the distance, but it's almost as if someone has been cleaning up their kills.

I quickly glance at Rian and I don't even have to say a word before she is pulling out the gun and holding it protectively in front of her. We are limited on bullets, but I am just thankful we are both armed.

I inhale deeply, touching the back of my pants to ensure the knife Rian stole from the Degenerates is still there. A feeling of uneasiness is washing over me like waves. A piercing noise attacks my ears, and then I hear a voice over what sounds like an intercom. "Drop your weapons."

Rian locks eyes with me in a panic.

They have seen Rian's gun at this moment, but no one knows I am armed with a knife, and I intend to keep it that way.

I nod at Rian slightly giving her the okay. She bends down, setting it onto the ground.

We have no idea what or who we are dealing with, and the possibility of them having us surrounded is too great to disobey their orders. I glance back at the biters I noticed earlier, taking note that they have closed quite a bit of distance on us. There is a group of five descending upon Rian and me, but I can't make any sudden movements. I have to keep my knife hidden. I swallow loudly, attempting to calm my rising heartbeat.

Bullets whiz past our faces as I notice all of the biters get taken out in one fell swoop. My heart is in my throat. My eyes scan the guard towers, but I still have limited visibility. Finally, I notice two males and a female approaching the gates from the inside. Two of them are carrying rifles. None of them are wearing military fatigues, and my bad feeling continues to intensify. The female is older, in her mid-forties with short blond hair and brown eyes. She has muscular arms and a prominent jawline. She is quite masculine looking. The two men are younger. One appears to be in his early thirties and Hispanic, while the other is probably no older than me and African-American. They look dirty, and none of them wear inviting expressions on their faces. In fact, the youngest of the three wears what appears to be a permanent scowl on his face.

Once they have us secured inside the gates, the older male turns to the other two. "Search them."

My heartbeat accelerates as I feel Rian glancing my way. There is no way they will overlook the knife now. I watch as the woman pats down Rian, and then the younger male approaches me. He takes his time running his hands up and down my legs. I can tell he is taking pleasure in his job. He slides his hand down the middle of my chest in between my breasts and lingers there. I want to kick him in the balls, but I already know we are in deeper than I'd like us to be. He circles around me to the back, and yet again takes the liberty of fondling my breasts during his search. I think I may get away with the knife tucked inside of the back of my pants, when his hands finally come into contact with it.

"What is this?" he asks in a sinister voice as he pulls it out slowly. I hear Rian gasp, and then I see the female grab her arms and hold her back. She is thrashing around in an attempt to free herself as the male who had been searching me brings the knife up to my throat.

"No!" Rian cries loudly, but I keep a poker face. Looking forward without bothering to lock eyes with the dirty scumbag.

"What's your name?" he asks into my ear, and I swear I can feel his tongue against my earlobe.

"Marley," I reply, silencing Rian with an icy stare.

"So, Marley, where you guys coming from?" The older man asks.

"Texas," I lie yet again.

"And who might you be?" the Hispanic male inches toward Rian.

"Bree," I answer for her. I got us into this mess. I want to keep all of the attention on me, if possible.

"Marley and Bree," he states, glancing between the both of us. "And you are?"

Jean-Luc peeks out from behind my back. "I'm Jean-Luc."

"Well, I'm Hector, and this is Linda and Doug."

Doug finally releases me, and Linda does the same with Rian. I quickly pull her into me, protectively. I don't like the look in Hector's eyes, it's just a bit too familiar. They keep their guns trained on us as they shuffle us into the prison. It is dingy and dirty, and there is an unhealthy ratio of men to women as we pass through one of the cell blocks. My thoughts are running wild.

What the hell did I get us into?

* * *

Although I know with everything in me that we are not safe, we are outnumbered and the only thing we can do at this point is to play nice. They set us up in our own cell and are surprisingly welcoming. They make sure we get something to eat and then later in the evening they even bring Rian and me tea. They split us up from Jean-Luc, but I try not to question their motives too much. Although they are being overly inviting, I still don't trust them as far as I can throw them, so I have no intention of sleeping. Rian passes out before she even finishes her tea, and I assume she's just that exhausted.

I have no intention of sleeping tonight. I have no idea who we are dealing with or even what. I don't trust anyone but Rian. She's been through enough, so I keep my suspicions to myself. She's only fourteen years old. She should be writing love letters to boys in school, not killing the undead and defending her life. What I would give to be able to give her a normal upbringing.

* * *

I don't remember passing out. All I know is something catches my ear, and my eyes fly open, my body shooting upright. I'm shaking uncontrollably, with sweat dripping down my forehead. My eyes scan my unfamiliar surroundings, and I realize I'm in a cell. I shift my eyes to the other cot in the room and it is empty. *Rian? Where is Rian?*

My eyes are still blurry as I make my way out into the cement hallway and slink down it, trying not to wake anyone. I hear faint voices, and what sounds like a struggle at the end of the dark, dimly lit pathway. My eyes adjust to the moonlight reflecting off the mirrors inside the bathroom, and I can now see Rian has been cornered by two guys, one of them being the Hispanic gentleman from earlier, and it does not look like a friendly conversation.

My heart drops. *This is not how she should be living her life.*

Get her out.

I know firsthand what the repercussions of what they are about to do to her will be. She won't be the same innocent girl ever again. Flashes of my horrific childhood flicker through my mind, and my breathing intensifies. Rage is pouring out of every orifice in my body. I'm on the back of the bigger one, punching and kicking him. My arms are wrapped around his throat and I can feel his fingers wrapped around my wrists, attempting to pry me off. He rams me into the wall roughly and pain shoots up my entire back. I cry out loudly.

Rian sinks her teeth into the other low life as he's too fixated on my scuffle, and he picks her up and throws her at an adjacent wall. Her body falls to the floor and she's unconscious. Everything is happening too quickly. *I can't protect her.*

I watch in slow motion as her attacker dives for a knife that is laying on the ground by the wall, and I shout out to him. "Hey, take one more step and I'll snap his neck." My hands are in the perfect position to get rid of his buddy for good, he's wiggling around, and trying to fight me off, but all it takes is one small movement...

"You're out of your league here," he hisses, and then flashes an evil smile at me. He's taken the knife to Rian's underwear, and I lose it.

Snap.

The bigger one goes down in an instant, me falling with him. I roll off quickly, and then kick my leg out, tripping Rian's attacker. He falls flat to the cement on his back, his head bouncing off the ground. He is scrambling to get to his feet, when I step on his wrist until he cries out in pain, releasing the knife. I swipe the knife quickly, and with no more thought, I stab him in the chest repeatedly. The blood splattering up and onto my face.

My heart begins to pulsate. *Thud. Thud. Thud.* I am beginning to come to terms with what I have just done. My fingers unclench from the knife dropping it onto the ground. I rush over to Rian's side, and attempt to wake her. She's just beginning to come to when I position her arm around my neck and stand. Earl comes barreling around the corner, and I am met with the greasy Degenerate face to face.

"Phoenix," Rian says weakly.

Earl's eyes begin to adjust as recognition takes over his face. His eyes go dark and sinister. "Code Red!" he screams out before I get a chance to react.

How the hell am I going to get us out of this?

Seven – Mixed Feelings

Ike

"I think you've got an admirer," Cullen states lazily from his position on his cot.

I swivel my head around and sure enough a small pair of eyes are peering back at me from the neighboring cell.

"Hello, Neveah, how are you doing today?" I say gently, standing up from my own cot and stepping closer to the bars.

She looks down, her eyes averting my gaze, but a smile plays upon her lips. She is the definition of adorable.

"You know I don't bite," I state, reaching my hand through the bars toward her.

She shies away still, but giggles this time. "Bet you can't find me!" she exclaims excitedly, and then races out of her cell and down the hall.

I chuckle lightly, turning back to look at Cullen.

"Well, what are you waiting for?" Cullen asks, setting the gun he's been cleaning down on the cot beside him.

I shake my head, smiling and then make my way out of the cell. "Marco," I call down the long hallway, my voice echoing off the concrete walls.

"Polo!" I hear far off in the distance. I make my way toward the noise, continuing to call out every few moments to make sure I am getting closer.

As I am passing by the mess hall, I see Carmen sitting alone at one of the tables, her nose in a book. Curiosity gets the better of me, and I enter swiftly, headed straight for her.

"Good morning, Ike," she greets me without bothering to look up from the book.

"Good morning," I reply, taking a seat on the bench across from her.

"What are you reading there?"

She lifts the book up so I can inspect the back cover.

"The Great Gatsby," I state once I've seen the familiar title. "That's a good one."

The corners of her lips pull up into a small

smile. "We have a pretty awesome library here. I try to read a couple of books a week."

I can't remember the last time I read a book simply for pleasure, but Carmen makes it look appealing.

"She been keeping you on your toes?" Carmen asks, turning the page.

I chuckle, remembering that I got off hand. "She's definitely a fire cracker. Does she get that from you?"

Carmen's smile widens as she finally puts the book down, her emerald eyes locking onto mine. "You could say that."

"Well, what else can you tell me about yourself?" I ask, intrigued.

She blushes slightly, tucking in her cheek. "What do you want to know?"

I shrug. "Who were you before all of this?"

She inhales deeply. "I was a nurse. I loved helping people. I loved making a difference."

Her answer only makes her more attractive in my eyes.

"What about you? What did you do?"

"I was a colonel in the United States military. I was in the middle of my fourth deployment when the virus got out."

She nods, listening. "What part of the military?"

"I was an infantryman."

Her eyebrows raise. "I knew you had to have been someone influential."

"What makes you say that?" I ask, curiously.

"The way you carry yourself. The way that you speak. You are very respectful, but I definitely feel a sense of leadership when it comes to you."

Her words make me smile unknowingly. She doesn't have a clue about the person I am, and yet she was able to gather that much from the brief time we've known one another.

"Polo!" I hear Neveah's loud call from down the hall.

"Well, I better get back to it then," I say, standing up from the table.

Carmen smiles, picking her book back up. "Don't let her tire you out, she has unlimited energy these days."

I chuckle as I spin around. "Good to know."

I know playing with Neveah won't make up for the terrible decisions I made when it came to my own family, but it will dull the pain. I will never be careless when it comes to the people I care about ever again. Phoenix, Rian, and Cullen have become my family, and I will do whatever it takes to keep them safe.

* * *

Cullen

Something is off here. Things are better than they should be. There's food, water, shelter. I'm having trouble believing that it can be *this* easy. Ike on the other hand is embracing it fully.

He's had a mini-shadow since we arrived. Neveah. A little girl not much older than his daughter was has been following him around. Her mother has light skin and emerald eyes with killer dimples. Her name is Carmen.

Ike definitely has a hard-on for Carmen and really likes Neveah. For the first time in a long time, he seems happy.

It's only been a week but I can tell Ike is settling in, feeling comfortable. I think we shouldn't let our guard down until we know their final agenda.

I'm sitting in the mess hall, eating, when something catches my attention. "I wonder what the other prison is like and what kind of pussy they have over there," a guy sitting across from me says.

My breath hitches. "You're telling me there is *another* prison? How far away is it?"

His eyes widen when he realizes this is news to me. "Not more than twenty miles away. In fact, I think it's even less than that." The way his eyes light up is sickening.

I snort unconsciously.

"But it's overrun with Degenerates," he says in a sing-song voice.

"How do you know that?" I ask.

"It's fact."

I bolt forward and wrap my fingers around his small throat, applying pressure. "How the hell do you know that?"

I can feel the eyes on me from all around the room. People look scared, frightened, frozen. And then there are the ones who are watching with fascination, envy, and jealousy.

"We've scoped it out," the guy chokes out.

I release my grip quickly, and then jump up, making a beeline for our sleeping quarters. Ike is lying on his cot when I make it there.

"Did you know?" I ask Ike angrily.

His eyes narrow and he sits up slowly. "Know what?"

I don't bother replying, but I assume he'll be able to tell what I'm talking about just from the daggers I'm shooting him from my eyes. He inhales deeply. "Yes."

I toss my cot upside down in a rage. "How long have you known?" I growl.

Ike has his hands up in surrender, and people are beginning to flock towards the entrance to our cell.

"A few days." I want to punch things, I want to hit things. His answer only makes it worse. "I'm sorry," Ike says quietly. "We are safe for the first time in as long as I can remember. We don't even know if they have Phoenix and Rian.

"Look, I don't give a fuck if you come with me or not, but I'm going," I say huffily before heading toward the crowd. I feel a hand grip my shoulder and pull me back.

"What's the plan?" he asks calmly.

Eight – The Pain of Living

Phoenix

We are surrounded. Now they just look like rabid beasts ready to tear us apart. Earl and Jerrica are leading the advance.

"You must love danger," Jerrica says.

We are weaponless and I know this is not going to end well for us.

My heart sinks lower into my stomach when someone reaches from behind me pulling Rian away and holding a knife across her throat.

"Let her go," I warn, my hands out, showing them I'm not a threat.

Jerrica cackles. "I heard this rumor somewhere that you two aren't even blood relatives. Is this true?"

I can feel the pressure around my heart, like someone is gripping it inside their palm, their fingers squeezing the life slowly out of me.

I shake my head. "Jerrica…" I can't lie to her now. Not when she knows the truth. Not when

Rian's life hangs in the balance.

"Answer the question," she pushes.

I nod slowly, remaining quiet.

"Well isn't that just a crying shame?" She smiles. "It's time for you to learn a lesson, my dear." She turns to the perpetrator holding Rian. "Toss her."

"No!" I don't think I've ever screamed louder in my life. I lunge toward Rian, but it's too late. There is a gash across her throat. Dark red blood is spilling out. Her eyes are rolling to the back of her head.

I'm hugging her to my chest, begging her to just hold on when the gun shots begin. They are right out the front doors, and they distract the crowd surrounding me.

Rian is gone. Her body is limp.

I have to move.

I maneuver my way out the opposite direction of the Degenerates and run smack dab into something firm. I swivel my head up, and my heart feels like a fish out of water. I let my eyes swoop over his face and mouth before meeting his.

Cullen.

His brow furrows in concern. "Phoenix, are you okay? Where's Rian?"

It's not until that moment that I realize my eyes are blurred with tears and I am gasping for breath. *I've lost my whole family.*

I don't have anyone.

When I fail to respond, understanding comes over his face. "Bloody hell. We need to get you out of here!"

"No!" I push him away from me angrily. I notice a pistol in his right hand and swipe it as quickly as possible.

"What the hell, Phoenix?" he barks, his eyes narrowing.

I can't think. I can't speak. The only thing I know is that I need to kill them. Every last one of them.

Jerrica and Earl are long gone at this point, but I race off in the direction I saw them go. Gunshots are ringing out all over the place, but I can't focus on that. Any familiar face I recognize as a Degenerate I take out. They don't even have a chance to part their lips to speak before I empty a round of bullets into their heads and bodies. I can hear Cullen behind me, screaming at me, but I ignore him.

I've taken out four Degenerates when I run out of bullets. Someone comes barreling around the corner, and I hold up my gun in the direction, knowing they have no idea I'm out. My heart stops when I realize it's Ike.

"Phoenix?" he asks, confusion spreading over his face. "What are you doing? Where is Rian?"

Rian. Rian. Fuck.

The desperation that crosses my face answers his question and his face falls. "No, no, no..." He is shaking his head, mumbling the words, looking down. My heart breaks even more. "Where is she?" he asks.

Cullen reaches a hand up to my shoulder from behind, I don't have to look back to see the sympathy in the depths of his eyes.

Ike pushes past both of us, rushing back toward Rian's lifeless body.

"Ike!" Cullen cries, chasing after him. Gunshots are still ringing out and I find myself torn. I need to avenge her death, but my friend needs me too. Neither will make me feel any better. Neither will bring her back to me.

My legs carry me back to the scene of the crime. Back to my sister's body splayed out in a pool of blood. Ike has her cradled against his body, and he is rocking back and forth, crying.

"Ike, Phoenix, we *need* to get out of here!" Cullen insists, his face contorts into a painful expression.

"We can't just leave her here," I say sharply.

Cullen sighs. He probably thinks I'm stupid. He probably thinks I have a death wish. But I'm already dead inside. Rian deserves a proper burial. If it's the last thing I do.

*   *   *

"Phoenix," Cullen says softly, placing his hand gently on my shoulder. "You should come inside."

I haven't moved an inch since we managed to make it back to the other prison. We buried her hours ago, but I haven't been able to move a muscle.

"What if she's cold?" I say through tears.

Cullen kneels beside me, his face fallen.

"Phoenix." The pity in his voice angers me. I hate people feeling sorry for me.

I bat his hand away from me. "I'm not leaving her!"

He looks hurt by my outburst, but I could care less. A few minutes later, I hear him stand and his footsteps back to the door. I don't move a muscle.

Eventually the sky darkens and the flood lights turn on, illuminating the prison yard. The temperature is dropping at a rapid pace, and the only thing I can think is that she's freezing. I remove my hoodie, placing it on top of the freshly dug grave. Goose bumps instantly rise on my body, but I ignore them. Instead I lay my head down on my sweatshirt, and cry myself to sleep.

* * *

When I awake, my eyes are sore from crying, they are raw. I realize almost immediately I am not outside. I bolt upright, realizing that someone carried me inside. I'm fuming. I begin stalking out of the unfamiliar prison cell when I feel someone reach out and grab my arm.

"Phoenix," it's Ike. I glance back seeing the redness of his cheeks, and I know he's been crying to. "Where are you going?"

"She's alone." I point toward the outside.

He takes a sharp, shaky intake of breath and I can see the pain in the depths of his hazel eyes. "This isn't easy for any of us."

I glare back at him. "You don't know what they did to her! You weren't there. I'm to blame. I'm the reason they killed her!"

I don't even realize I'm screaming until Cullen has woken up and is beside me. I can feel a plethora of eyes on us, and I become instantly uncomfortable. I high-tail it out of the cell, and outside the cement walls. The cold wind roughly whips my face as I make it outside, and I rush over to the area where I last left her. The sun is just beginning to rise in the sky, and judging by the dark clouds, I'd guess it's about to rain.

I fall to the ground beside the makeshift grave, tears making it difficult to see. "I'm sorry. I'm so, so sorry I didn't protect you."

I breathe in deeply. "I would give anything in the world to trade places with you right now. My entire life, the only thing I've ever tasked myself to do was to protect you, and I failed. I failed you."

I'm sobbing now, the tears raking through my body violently. I am gripping my sides tightly, my head and eyes downcast. I feel a drop on my head and I look up through swollen eyes to see the first raindrops emerging from the dark clouds.

I hear the door open and footsteps making their way toward me, but I don't look his way. I know it's Cullen. The rain begins to pelt the ground faster and harder, but still I remain firmly planted. I bring my knees up to my chin and wrap my arms around them tightly, rocking back and forth.

Cullen never leaves my side. He doesn't say a word, just sits with me so I'm not alone.

I'm shivering from the rain and the cold temperatures, but I manage to drift off, my head in Cullen's lap. It's a time for me to momentarily forget that I've lost Rian forever. A few hours later, I wake up in Cullen's arms as he carries me throughout the prison. I don't bother fighting him this time, I'm too exhausted.

He takes me into the bathroom of the prison and strips me of my soaked clothes. He doesn't pressure me to speak, instead he carries my naked body into the shower and puts me under the faucet, the hot water beating down on me.

A few minutes later, once he's stripped himself of his own clothes, he joins me, wrapping his arms around my body. We just stay like that, under the showerhead until the water goes cold. Until our skin is wrinkled and prune-like.

He dries me off, rubbing the towel over my bare skin and wet hair, and then he helps me into new, dry clothes. I am now in an orange prison shirt and pants. After redressing himself, he pulls me through the prison by my hand, stopping only once to drop off our wet clothes.

"Thanks, Carmen," I hear him say, and then he begins tugging on my hand again.

I'm finding it hard to find the energy to breathe.

I wish I hadn't woken up. Just stayed in that dream world.

Cullen shows me back to the cell I had my screaming fit in less than eight hours ago, and helps me onto the uncomfortable bed, covering me with a thin blanket. He lays down behind me, his arm reaching around, and pulling me in tighter to him.

I feel empty. I feel dead.

I feel his free hand gently moving hair out of my face and tucking it behind my ear. I want to cry, but it's physically impossible. My tear ducts are overworked and dried up. So instead I just lay there in silence, blinking away the pain.

Nine – An Attempt to Move On

Ike

Things have been…difficult since Rian. Not only for Phoenix, but for all of us. Rian completed the group. She was one of us, and now she's gone. First Foster, and now her. I'm not sure we can handle another loss. Neither Cullen nor I have been able to have the conversation with Phoenix about Foster. Not now. The loss of Rian is too fresh, and Phoenix is too unstable. I know we are eventually going to have to break the news. I'm not looking forward to it in the least.

I've been helping out with more of the chores around the prison. I've found that keeping myself busy keeps my mind preoccupied. As it turns out, all of us grieve in different ways. Cullen hasn't left Phoenix's side. She's lucky to have him.

Winter is slowly sneaking upon us, and the nights are getting colder. Luckily, we still have electricity, so we've been utilizing the heat quite a bit. But the concrete floors and cement walls are still much too cold when the sun goes down.

I've been working in the kitchen this week, helping prepare the meals. I was never much of a cook in my previous life, but I've been enjoying creating new concoctions. I've gotten multiple compliments this week on the food, so I think I'm doing something right. Today, I'm preparing a beef stew. We have enough food to last us for another month or so, but I know our supplies are running low. Given how many people reside inside these walls, it's been leaving me with an uneasy feeling in the pit of my stomach.

"Hey you." Carmen pokes her head into the kitchen, her emerald eyes peeking at me.

"Hey," I greet her with a small smile.

"That smells good." She takes a few more steps into the kitchen area and I can now see she is wearing a light yellow dress and a tan shall. She looks absolutely stunning. Her beauty takes my breath away most days, but today it's ten-fold.

"You look nice," I compliment her, still giving her the once over. "But aren't you cold?"

She cracks a smile. "Thank you. We never have a reason to dress up anymore, so I thought it might be nice to pretend for a few hours."

I chuckle lightly. "Good for you."

She inches closer to me, eyeing the large crockpot in front of me. "That smells nice. What are you cooking for us today?"

I take the lid off, the steam rising into the air and our nostrils. "Beef stew."

She revels in the savory smell. "Do you need any help?"

I glance back over at her attire. "I'm not sure you're dressed to be helping in the kitchen."

She looks back down at her dress and then back up at me. "Seriously? Who cares about getting a little dirty these days?" She walks behind me to the wall, grabs one of the black aprons and tosses it over her head, tying it in the back. "Tell me what you need me to do."

Normally there is a handful of people helping in the kitchen, but with everything going on, I gave the rest of the workers the day off. I know it's a large order for me to cook enough food for everyone, but I was enjoying my solitude.

"Why don't you cut up those carrots?" I motion with my head toward the stack of carrots lying on the cutting board.

She slides past me, headed for them, and our arms graze. My heartbeat instantly begins to beat faster. Carmen is without a doubt, a gorgeous woman, but part of me feels guilty. I was with my wife for fifteen years. I don't know if it is too soon to be thinking of another woman in such a way. I never thought I'd ever be in such a predicament.

"Look," Carmen says, when there's been more than a few minutes of silence filling the air. "I haven't wanted to overstep, so I've been distant these past couple of days, but are you okay?"

I stop peeling the potato I'm holding and glance at her.

"I don't know the details of what happened, but I do know what it feels like to lose someone, so if you ever need someone to talk to, I'm here," she offers with a small smile before returning to chopping up the carrots.

I inhale sharply. "Thank you." I'm not sure I'm ready to talk about it, but her concern does make me feel a bit better.

"I like you, Ike, and I know that may be forward of me to just come out and say, but you're a good person. You're good with Neveah, you're good with the people here, you're just good all the way around. I'd really like the chance to get to know you better…if you're interested," she says.

I swallow, digesting her words. *I used to be a good person…now I'm not so sure anymore.* "Carmen," I say through a shaky breath. "I don't know how to do this. I never thought I'd ever be in this position again in my life. I met my wife when I was in high school, our families grew up together, and we went to the same school, same church. Everything just fell into place. I don't even know if I understand the concept of dating, much less flirting."

She nods her head in understanding. "We've all been through things we never imagined we'd have to face, but we're here now. I don't know what tomorrow holds, and I sure as hell don't know if we're doing right by our beloved spouses…but, I know I like you, and I'm interested enough to see where this goes."

I stop what I'm doing, facing her fully now. As much as I want to entertain her words, I know I don't deserve happiness. Not after what I did to my own family. Carmen deserves someone much better than me. "I'm flattered, Carmen, I am. You're gorgeous, you're funny, and you're genuine, three things that anyone would be lucky to find…but I'm not the person you think I am. I've made mistakes, a lot of them, and after everything, I don't deserve you."

Carmen drops the knife she's holding on to the cutting board abruptly, and then gets up into my face. She is shorter than me, but she's invaded my personal bubble, so much so that I have unintentionally retreated back to the adjacent wall, my back pressed up against it. My heart is thumping against my ribcage madly. At first I think I've angered her, but the look in her emerald eyes tells me another story. She stands up on her tip-toes and slowly leans in, gently pressing her lips against mine. I'm in shock at first, I forget to close my eyes, but they flutter closed as I deepen the kiss. There is a flame coursing through my entire body. It's something I used to feel the first few years with my wife whenever we kissed. I never thought I'd ever feel it again.

I bring my hand up to her face, cradling it as the kiss continues. She runs her tongue across my bottom lip, and I almost lose it all.

"Oh, I'm sorry..." I hear someone say and then a shuffle of footsteps out of the kitchen.

I break the kiss off, breathing heavily, and looking towards the entrance. Whoever it was is long gone by now. I glance back at Carmen, and she is removing her apron and hanging it back on the wall.

"I'm going to be in the library tonight, working.

You should come by," she says, and then slides past me and out of the kitchen. My mind is reeling from the stolen kiss. A million different emotions are shooting through me at top speed. As much as I want to dissect what just happened, I know I have to finish cooking. I can mull it all over later.

* * *

"Where is he?" Phoenix asks, a frantic look covering her face. She has run into the kitchen as I am dishing up the beef stew, Cullen in tow.

I glance at Cullen and his face falls, letting me know he hasn't had a chance to discuss what happened to Foster with her yet.

I sigh looking at one of my helpers in the kitchen. "Can you take over for a moment?"

The teenage boy looks back at me, his shaggy blond hair obscuring his eyes and nods. I remove my apron and hang it up on the wall. "Let's chat back in our cell."

"No!" Phoenix cries. "I'm tired of you guys treating me like I'm some kind of baby. Where is Foster?"

Cullen's facial expression falls, and she catches it. "No!" she cries. "Foster!" She takes off, running throughout the prison, calling his name, and looking in each and every cell block. When she makes it to solitary, she falls to the ground, wailing.

They don't keep anyone in the solitary confinement wing, so luckily her breakdown is only in our presence. "What happened to him?" she asks through tears, gripping her sides for support.

Cullen and I help her to her feet. "Degenerates," Cullen replies simply.

Phoenix's eyes go dark, and I know it isn't good. "They can't get away with it. They think they're gods...that their actions have no consequences?" She shakes her head angrily. "I'm going to make them pay."

She pulls away from the both of us, headed straight for the weapons room. "Phoenix! Phoenix!" we call after her, but she ignores our pleas as she barges into the room.

Pauly is sitting, his head in a magazine and his legs crisscrossed on top of a desk. He slowly sets down the automobile magazine, and shifts his green eyes toward Phoenix.

"I need a gun," she tells him.

He looks at her tear-stricken face, and then past her at Cullen and me. "Alright, what for?"

We are shaking our heads furiously, both knowing this move could get us all killed.

"I need it for protection," she lies.

Pauly again looks to us for confirmation. We are both motioning that this is a bad idea without saying a word. We know Phoenix would be livid with us if she knew the truth.

Pauly sighs, standing up and walking toward the front of the desk. "Look, I'm not sure what's going on, but it looks like you might be a little upset, and we can't chance you making a rash decision with a firearm."

Phoenix snorts. "What is wrong with all of you people?" she exclaims angrily. "All you want to do is play house while the Degenerates are out there killing innocent people!"

Pauly's facial expression changes, first to sympathy and then to understanding. "Look, I understand why you're upset, but we have to be conscientious of our ammo."

Phoenix grunts before she goes barreling out of the room and down the hallway. Cullen and I glance at one another, sharing an understanding before he goes racing off after her. I stay behind, turning my attention back on Pauly. "Thank you."

He shrugs. "No problem, Ike. You've been a big help around here, and you know any time you want to check out a weapon, it's yours."

I nod. "Thank you."

He motions with his head toward the door. "She going to be okay?"

I sigh, my shoulders falling. "Not anytime soon, but she will be."

* * *

My palms are sweating, my breathing is shallow, and my heart is beating erratically. I straighten the sweater I am wearing, and continue looking down at my feet attempting to regulate my breathing.

"You know you have nothing to be worried about, right?" Cullen chuckles from behind me.

I sigh. "I haven't done this in over a decade. I'm just a little rusty."

We are in the bathroom in front of the mirrors.

I had to tell someone about what happened earlier, so I decided to confide in Cullen. When I told him I wasn't planning on going, he practically punched me. Since then, he managed to find me a nice sweater in my size, and convince me to go.

Cullen spins me around so we are facing one another. "It's just like riding a bike. It will all come back to you."

I take a deep breath in, my eyes falling back to the floor.

"Look," Cullen says softly, his hands still on my shoulders. "Just because you're doing this doesn't mean Robyn and Asia mean any less to you. They would want you to be happy, Ike."

Tears sting the corner of my eyes. "They deserve to be here," I choke out.

Cullen sighs. "Without a doubt, but you can't keep living your life in the past. They wouldn't want that for you."

I hear every word he says, but it doesn't make it any easier.

"Look, I have to get back to Phoenix, but you got this." He slaps me on the shoulder and then begins making his way out of the bathroom.

I exhale sharply, his words echoing in my mind. *You got this.*

I'm a nervous wreck when I make it to the library. The door is nearly closed, so I push it open lightly, peeking my head in. The lights are dim, and only one lamp is on illuminating a small area in the back of the room. I let myself in, closing the door softly behind me. "Carmen?" I call out.

"Back here," her voice floats from the back of the room.

I walk toward the lamp, and sure enough she is sprawled out in a chair, a book in her hands. A smile breaks out onto her lips when I approach. "I wasn't sure you'd come."

I rub my hand over my head. "I wasn't sure I should."

She sets the book down on the ground and stands up, inching toward me. "It's okay to be nervous. I am."

I gulp. "You are?"

She nods, her eyes dancing. "You're not the only one who's out of practice."

I swallow as I realize maybe I have been

overthinking it all.

She glances at the sweater I am wearing. "This new?"

I chuckle. "New to me."

She slides a finger across the fabric, my heartbeat intensifying from the slight touch. "It looks nice."

"Thank you," I reply. "Where's Neveah?" I look around the empty library.

"Karen is watching her. She does that from time to time for me."

I nod, feeling the pressure begin to build up inside of me.

She smiles back at me. "You know, we don't have to do anything you're not comfortable with. I just want to spend time with you."

Her words bring me comfort. Everything had moved so fast in the kitchen, I wasn't sure what she was expecting from me tonight. "Yeah?" I ask.

She nods. "Yeah." She walks over to a small table in the middle of the room and pulls out a chair, seating herself. She pats the seat across from her. "Sit."

We talk for the next few hours, and it's more than I could have ever hoped for. She doesn't pressure me, and the conversation flows effortlessly. When she yawns, I realize that it's probably time to let her get back to her daughter. "This was nice," I say softly, standing.

"Yeah," she agrees smiling up at me.

"I'd like to do it again sometime..." I trail off, unsure how she feels.

She steps toward me. "Me too," she murmurs. The way she is looking at me, and the way the light bounces off her yellow dress leaves me speechless. Before I fully comprehend what I am doing, I am leaning down, pressing my lips to hers.

In a perfect world, this moment would be shared with my wife, but in the world we live in now, I can't imagine a more perfect moment.

Ten – Glimpses of a Simpler Time

Cullen

It's difficult seeing Phoenix like this. She's broken, and I can't do anything to help. I know that she would have given anything to save Rian. She's allowing her guilt to win, letting it eat her alive. She's been her own form of zombie the past couple of days. All she does is sleep and eat.

I want to let her know that I am here for her, but I don't want her to think I have ill intentions. I just wish I could make her see that she isn't alone.

Jerrica is still alive somewhere, and I know Phoenix is plotting her revenge fantasy. I can see it in her eyes. With the knowledge she has of Foster's death, her disdain for the Degenerates grows. I wasn't sure she could hate them anymore than she already did. I was wrong.

Ike is taking losing Rian pretty hard as well. I think it is making him relive what happened with his wife and daughter, and I can tell it's taking a toll on him.

It's been pouring down rain for the past two days. We've been cooped up inside, staying warm and dry. I head toward the bed Phoenix has been spread out on, and Ike greets me.

"Hey Cullen," he says softly, standing up to meet me at eye level.

I look around his head and to the empty cot. "Where is she?"

He takes a small step backward, raising his hands. "Don't be mad, she's doing what she has to."

I inhale sharply. "What the hell does that mean, and why do I get the feeling that it's not good for any of us?"

He shrugs. "Come on, I can take you to her."

I follow him through the hallways until we enter a room that was probably used as the infirmary back when it was open. Phoenix is lying flat down on one of the metal carts. A needle is placed into her arm and a blood bag is filling. "What's going on?" I ask, taking a step toward her.

Jean-Luc shuffles toward me. "We need her blood to be able to manufacture the cure."

My eyes dart between the two before landing on her blue ones.

"Are you sure you are up for this right now?" I ask gently, taking another step closer.

She nods weakly, traces of tears down her cheeks, leaving a rosy tint. I rub my finger over her cheek. "You know, it's okay to be sad."

She nods, squeezing her eyes closed and inhaling deeply. "We don't have time for sadness. What we need is a leader."

I hear Ike suck in his breath behind me and realize I had forgotten he was even in the room. I'm not sure how much he liked her leader comment.

"What do you plan to do with the cure once you do have it?" I address the question to both Jean-Luc and Phoenix.

Phoenix grins a sly smile at me. "It's going to be our new bargaining chip."

I nod. "I like the way you think."

* * *

I awake with a jolt, falling straight out of the bed, and onto the concrete floor with a thud.

It's a wakeup call. My eyes travel over to where Phoenix should be asleep, and she's nowhere in sight. I stumble up, grabbing my knife while I'm at it. Ike is snoring lightly, so I remain quiet, not wanting to wake him unless absolutely necessary.

I peek out into the hall, and can now clearly hear the sounds of sleep coming from all around me. I walk slowly and quietly until I make it out the front door and outside. It's pitch dark outside, but the flood lights illuminate the dirty ground beneath me. The light ricochets off the metal gate, establishing a pathway. The rain has lightened up. It smells fresh and clean, and sprinkles the ground.

There is groaning and teeth chattering along the edges of the gates. I can feel them reaching out for me as I walk hesitantly toward the side of the building. It doesn't take much to find her. She's hovered over Rian's grave, her arms crossed around her body. I'm not sure how long she's been outside, but her clothing is soaked, and her stature tells me that she is crying.

"Phoenix," I say softly as I reach out for her.

She swivels around and stands up, swinging her arms away from her body.

"Phoenix," I say yet again, unsure of how I should be approaching her.

"I'm fine, Cullen," she says shortly but her expression and the way her lip quivers tell me a different story.

I take a slow, yet deliberate step toward her, my heart beating loudly inside of my chest. *God, I've missed you.* It's a strange thought to have, but I do. I miss her even when I am with her. I barely know her, and yet, I've missed those eyes, that hair, that resting bitch face.

"You don't look fine," I state.

She rolls her eyes dramatically. "You don't know me."

I exhale slowly. "No, I don't. But, I want to."

I see a sliver of something pass across her eyes, and then pain registers once more. "Why'd you leave?" her voice is so low, I have to strain to hear it.

Guilt washes over me. "I shouldn't have. I made a mistake. I'm so sorry."

She stifles a sob, and then falls into my shoulder. I am slow pulling her in, she's been so guarded, so private, and I don't want to scare her away by moving too fast. I stroke her hair gently as I feel her breathing slow. I find myself lost in the moment, and it's over too quickly. I don't ever want to forget what it felt like having her in my arms.

"Rian was the only one in my family that accepted me for me. She was the only one who made me feel like I belonged anywhere. There was always a disconnect between my parents and me. I was the rebellious one of the family, constantly finding myself in trouble, constantly being punished for my stupid decisions. Rian covered for me so many times. I know I was the reason she ended up in boarding school. I didn't lead by the best example. But Rian, she loved me, and I loved her," Phoenix says in a small, shaky voice. "I mean, I had my brother, but we fought more than we ever got along. My mother used to say it was because we were so much alike...but I never felt that way. Rian was my mini-me. She idolized me. If I was like anyone, it was her. She made me a better person."

I'm surprised Phoenix has opened up to me in this moment, I don't want to ruin it by saying anything. If anything, I want her to continue. I want to hear more about her life before all of this chaos.

"And now that she is gone...I have no one,"

Phoenix says barely above a whisper.

I grip her face in between my hands, caressing it. "You have me."

Phoenix nods, she leans in gripping the collar of my sweatshirt, pulling my neck in close to her mouth. The warm breath tickling my skin is sending my body into overdrive.

I pull back, and then appreciate the way she is so vulnerable with me before leaning in and pressing my lips to hers. I know this isn't exactly the right time, but it feels too wrong to ignore.

She seems surprised, but she is aggressively kissing me back. She's biting my lip, sucking on it, and I can feel myself growing hard. Wind slaps me in the face coldly, and I remember where we are. I pull away from her, slowly. "Come on, let's go back inside."

She nods and then takes one step toward the door before spinning back around. "Don't you ever leave me again."

I stop breathing for a moment. "I won't baby, I promise."

She squeezes my hand once, and then pulls me back inside with her.

* * *

I wasn't sure it could happen, but things are finally getting easier. Phoenix still has her tough times, but they are less and less each day. The first week after losing Rian, she went off the rails, and I was scared I wouldn't be able to reel her back in, but she proved once more just how incredibly strong she actually is.

She's been helping out with the guard crew outside, the ones that kill the biters who line our fences. I think it's been helping her release her pent up aggression. She isn't so focused on a death mission anymore. Although, I know if given the chance, she'd take it.

I find her outside with little effort. "Hey, love." I kiss her on the top of her head in greeting as I watch her stab a biter through the fence.

"Hey you," she replies, shooting me a small smile. It's enough to make my heart flutter. It's funny how such a small gesture can affect me in such a big way, but that's how it is with her. Everything is enhanced, illuminated. My feelings are so much stronger for her than they've ever been for any woman that came before. Sometimes I wonder if it's because of the things we have been through together or if it's simply because of the person she is.

"You think you've had enough of this for one day?" I ask, motioning with my head toward the horde of biters outside the fence.

She smiles. "Maybe. What did you have in mind?"

I tilt my head to the side, pretending to be deep in thought. "I don't know...I just thought maybe we could spend a little time together. You know, without prying eyes."

She raises her eyebrows, her smile widening. "Yeah, maybe we could do that."

I grin back at her and then grab her hand, pulling her back inside with me. Because there are so many people within the confines of the walls, it's virtually impossible to get alone time, but I worked out a deal with Ike's new love interest that we could have free reign on the library for an hour, and I intend to utilize every minute.

Phoenix has a befuddled expression on her face when I pull her into the book-filled room. "This is so not what I had in mind." Her eyes scan the shelves dramatically.

I chuckle. "Listen, we're working with all we've got at the moment."

She sits on the edge of one of the tables in the room. "So...what do you want to do?"

I make my way to her, eyeing her up and down. I don't even bother answering, instead I decide to let our lips do the talking. I position myself in between her legs and lower my lips to hers in a passionate kiss. She kisses me back with eagerness and enthusiasm, and I'm happy that she's finally feeling somewhat normal again.

I take her bottom lip in mine, sucking it tenderly and then biting down on it gently. She moans in my mouth and my hand instantly goes to the back of her head, deepening our kiss. Her tongue slides along my bottom lip, wanting access inside. I oblige and our tongues meet, dancing with one another. She takes the tip of my tongue between her teeth gingerly, sucking on it. I pull away, panting. "Bloody hell, Phoenix. Where did you learn to do that?"

She smiles back at me seductively. "What?"

"You know exactly what I'm talking about. I rather fancied that."

She giggles. "You what?"

I shake my head, dropping it between her breasts, breathing heavily. "Now you've got me all worked up."

She reaches for the button on my pants when I stop her. "What are you doing?"

Her eyebrow raises. "I was going to help you out."

She doesn't have to elaborate, I know exactly what she means by it, and as incredible as it sounds, I'm not sure she's ready for that yet. Instead, I wrap my hand gently around her neck, pushing her down on the table so she is lying. Her eyes widen, but she bites her lip playfully in anticipation. I kiss her quickly before moving my lips to her neck and kissing her gingerly there. She closes her eyes, enjoying the simple touch of my mouth against her skin. My hand trails down her body, toward her thigh and I run it over the crotch of her pants.

"Let me spoil you," I whisper into her ear, before I begin removing her bottoms. I know we don't have much time left, but I plan on spoiling her in every way possible until the very last second.

Eleven – Falling into Routine

Ike

"Mr. Glass, are you awake?" I feel a slight tug on my hand. "Mr. Glass?" her high-pitched voice rings through once more.

I breathe in deeply, and then slowly allow my eyes to open. "Good morning to you too, Neveah."

It's strange to think that this has become routine for me. That we've been in the same place long enough for it to feel like home. I've been on the move since the outbreak, it's nice to not feel like I'm running from anything. I know the Degenerates will come looking for Phoenix, eventually, but for now, waking up ain't so hard anymore.

Her emerald eyes stare into mine intently. "Where's your mother?" I ask as I swing my legs around, and place them onto the cold ground.

She shrugs. "I think she's outside."

I run my hand over my eyes quickly, trying to rub the sleep away. "Was there something you needed?"

She cocks her head to the side playfully. "Mr. Glass, what does DILF mean?"

I about choke on my surprise when the abbreviated word comes out of her mouth. "What?"

She swings her arms around her body, nervously. "Why does my mom call you that?"

I can't help the chuckle that escapes my lips. "I don't know, why don't we ask her?"

Neveah glances up quickly to find her mother in the doorway, leaning against it.

"Ask me what?" she questions, locking her emerald eyes onto mine.

My heart begins doing a weird flopping thing inside my body, and it makes me feel guiltier than anything. I loved my wife. I still love my wife. I don't know what is right or wrong anymore.

I exhale deeply. I'm not sure I should do this, but I've already begun. "Neveah says you call me a DILF and we're both confused as to what you mean by it. Care to explain?"

Her cheeks grow rosy in an instant, and I can tell she isn't prepared to fire back. "Umm, uh," she stutters. She looks like she is about to leave us both high and dry, so I take a step toward her.

I break out into a round of laughter, throwing my head back for effect. "So, who's ready for breakfast?"

*   *   *

"So, how do we want to go about this?" I ask as Jean-Luc hands each of us a vial with the antiserum he's created to battle the infection.

"Well, we need a way to get the word out. We need to find the President of the United States. We have to find out how to get a mass message across," Phoenix chimes in, rolling the vile of blood between her fingers.

"We don't even know if the President is still in Washington. For all we know, they've taken him near the scene of the crime, and locked him up in Area 51." I like to think I am the voice of reason.

"I'll go," Cullen pipes up.

My eyes lock onto his. "Then I can come with

you."

He shakes his head dismissively. "No, you should stay here. Neveah and Carmen, they look up to you. They rely on you. I will be fine on my own."

Phoenix's eyes widen. "Hell no you won't. I'm coming with you."

Cullen backs up in surrender. "Okay, okay, you can come."

"You should take Jean-Luc with you," I state.

Cullen shakes his head dismissively. "It's hard enough trying to protect ourselves, but if anything happens to him, we won't have a way to continue making the antiserum. He has protection inside these walls that we can't guarantee on the outside."

"Do you really think it's smart to split up?" I ask the question that I'm sure is on everyone's mind.

Cullen shrugs. "We don't really have a choice, Ike. It would make no sense to leave this place, it's guaranteed safety, but if we want a chance to return the world to how it used to be, now is our chance."

He's right. Something about it just seems off though. Maybe it's because he's only been back for a little while.

"Here." Phoenix hands me two more vials of her blood. "Take extras. You have others to protect now." She closes her hands over mine, and then smiles up at me. "I'm going to miss you, old man."

I snort. "Old man? Who you calling old man? I'm still young and charming!"

She looks sad for a brief second before throwing her arms around me and squeezing. "This isn't the end. We're coming back for you."

I breathe in deeply. "Go save the world, sweet girl."

She pulls away and then feigns a smile. "You ready for this, Cullen?"

He takes a step toward her. "Ready."

Phoenix is carrying five vials of her blood, while Cullen is carrying an additional dozen. It won't be enough to save everyone, but it's a start.

* * *

Cullen

The first snow of the season has laid its path as we make our way on foot in the direction of Washington. We've been on the lookout for a means of transportation as it's too cold to be out and about, and it would be a hell of a lot quicker. Unfortunately for us, we haven't seen one in miles. At least not a viable option that isn't out of gas, or actually works.

Our trek on foot actually allows us more time to ponder over the future and what it will be like. Besides our chattering teeth, it's eerily quiet. Not more than a couple of biters in any direction. I wonder if we do make it to the President, how he will decide to rectify the situation. The infection has reached far beyond what we could have ever imagined by this point and it's going to be a long road ahead of us.

"Come here," I say quietly as I close the distance between myself and Phoenix. It's apparent she is freezing, so I wrap my arm around her shoulder and pull her in close.

"What is this for?" she asks, surprised by my gesture.

"If your teeth chatter any louder you're going to break them. Stop being stubborn and just enjoy the warmth I'm sharing with you," I order her.

She rolls her eyes. "Oh, please. You are just as cold as I am, and I'm betting you've been wanting to do this for a while now."

Her breath comes out with her words, and I chuckle. "Alright, you caught me. What can I say?"

She breaks apart from me and lunges forward, stabbing a biter in the skull. It falls limply to the ground after Phoenix pries the knife out.

I look up at the sky and see that we are running out of time. Soon it's going to be nightfall, and this area is going to be crawling with biters. We need to find a vehicle or shelter for the night.

"I know," Phoenix says, reading my mind. "I've got my eyes peeled."

Between the snow falling delicately from the sky, and the slight breeze, visibility is starting to become an issue.

I see Phoenix race forward, and for a moment, I lose sight of her. "Phoenix? Phoenix?" I cry out, my eyes darting back and forth between the snowflakes.

"There!" I hear her exclaim.

I take big strides to meet her and see exactly what she is referring to. It looks to be the remnants of a 7-11. All of the windows are smashed in and the place looks trashed. Lights are hanging loosely by wires, which are swinging back and forth as if someone knocked them recently.

"Uh, are you feeling alright?" I ask, unsure of what she could possibly see in the place.

She spins around, throwing her arms out. "I can hear them coming. We haven't seen anything else for miles. I think we're limited on options here."

I look back at the sad looking building, and then my eyes wander to the top. Of course. The roof. I lead the way into the store, trying to avoid stepping on the broken glass that is scattered across the floor. I hold up my knife, ready for anything that may jump out and surprise us. Phoenix is close behind, taking out a couple of biters every few moments, as I try to maneuver around as best as I can in the dark.

In what feels to be a storage closet, I run my hands along the walls and the countertops in search of anything we may be able to use. Phoenix follows suit. I almost trip over something large and metal, when I realize it's a ladder. *Bingo.*

"You're going to have to take point on this so I can get the ladder set up," I tell Phoenix. I reach along the walls, attempting to locate a switch for the lights, but after stumbling along for too many moments, I give up.

I can hear her shuffling around in the dark next to me, but can't see her. "Ladder?" she asks, confused.

"Yep, and we're going to need to find the back door and soon." I tuck the ladder under my arm, but with it being so dark I keep running into things, and end up making a lot more noise than I thought I might.

I can now hear the shuffling of feet, but I hope Phoenix has it covered. I hear a commotion, and possibly a struggle, and then a body falling to the ground. I hope it's not her.

I somehow make my way along the back wall and locate a back door that I assume was only accessed by employees during the lifetime of this convenience store. I push open the door, and can now see a few biters mulling about outside. The moonlight ricochets off the black asphalt, and gives me a sense of relief that I'm not fighting blind anymore. I had to pocket my knife earlier so that I could carry the damn thing, and now I have nothing to defend myself with. I toy with the idea of dropping the ladder and grabbing my knife, but I know we are limited on time, so I work with what I have.

I swing the ladder in a 360 degree circle, taking out three biters in one fell swoop. They all fall to the ground from the impact. They aren't dead, but I've at the very least, slowed them down. I drop the ladder quickly, positioning it as close to the side of the building as humanly possible. The biters I knocked down are already beginning to rise again, so I take a moment to take them down, one at a time; one stab to the head.

Phoenix is finally making her way outside, breathing heavily and I feel guilty that I left her in there all alone, but she's a firecracker, and I knew she could handle herself.

She glances up at the ladder quickly, and then back at me. "Well, what are we waiting on?"

"I was waiting on you, darling. Go ahead." I usher her up the stairs of the wobbly ladder, as I hold the base in place. I can hear a biter closing in, so once I see her step over the ledge and onto the roof, I turn around and stab the bloody thing in the eye. It goes down without much of a fight.

I hastily make my way up the ladder, when I feel resistance from the bottom, and notice biters are now making their way to the base. I can feel their arms reaching out for me. Fingers wrap around my ankle, trying to pull me downward. I kick aimlessly, hoping that it will be enough to wriggle free. My foot collides with what I assume to be a head, and I hear a loud thud at the bottom of the ladder.

"Here! Grab my hand!" Phoenix exclaims, reaching her hand over the side of the building. I take her small hand in mine, and we work together to get me over and off of the ladder. When I am finally on the roof, we look over the edge and notice the biters are beginning to understand how to climb the ladder and it's not the best situation for us.

I glance at Phoenix. "What do we do?" she asks, worriedly.

I look back down at the ladder. "We're going to need a way down. We need it."

She nods, gulping.

"Follow my lead," I order. I grab one side of the ladder as Phoenix grabs the opposite. There are now two biters ascending from the bottom of it, and they are halfway up. Other biters are beginning to crowd around the base. "Whatever you do, don't let go."

I begin tipping the top of the ladder toward the ground and back again, trying to shake off the two on it. One loses its balance, and falls the short distance to the ground, but the other, seems unfazed.

Phoenix glances at me, a stressed look playing upon her face. "What now?"

I can feel resistance from the bottom of the ladder. More hands are reaching for it than before. "One more time," I order as I roughly tip the ladder toward the ground, and then slam it back at the building. The second biter falls onto the crowd below, and I know this is our chance. "Now!" I shout at Phoenix, although she is right next to me. Probably the adrenaline kicking in. We both pull the ladder up with all of our might, and are able to free it from the prying hands below. We end up falling backwards onto the roof, the ladder landing right on top of us. We are both breathing heavily, attempting to catch our breath.

I stand back up, tossing the ladder off of us, before I extend out a hand to help Phoenix up. She dusts off her pants, before walking over to the edge where the ladder had previously been. She leans over the edge, looking down. "Shit, that was fast."

I follow her lead and am surprised to see a

horde of biters all pounding and grabbing at the brick building beneath us. My eyes scan the rest of the land around the building, and I can see the biters are coming out of the woodwork. They are all being attracted to the noise we've been making. I'm thankful we found a solution when we did.

I remove the backpack I've been carrying, dropping it to the ground, and opening it quickly, making sure I didn't damage any of the vials in my fall. Nothing looks awry, and I chalk it up to the fact that I was smart enough to pack one of the small, thin blankets from the prison alongside them.

I flash a dashing smile at Phoenix. "Well, might as well make yourself comfortable. We're going to be here awhile."

Twelve – The Advantages of Body Heat

Cullen

Night falls and the temperature drops even lower. I'm freezing myself, but the noise from Phoenix's teeth chattering is giving me one hell of a headache. She has her arms wrapped tightly around her body, and the hood of her sweatshirt is covering her head. I wrapped the blanket around her long ago, but it's too cold to sleep. The only thing I can think about is how bloody cold I am. "Come here," I say through chapped lips.

She lifts her head up slightly, locking her blue eyes onto mine. "What?" she barely gets out through all the chattering.

"You're freezing, I'm freezing, come here," I order once again.

She doesn't bother with a combative response as she stands up shakily, carrying the blanket with her, and closes the distance between us. I can finally make out the definition of her face as she nears, and it's obvious she is not only cold, but also exhausted and hungry. My own stomach growls loudly, and I'm reminded that

I can't even remember the last time I ate. I can tell my energy is lower, and starvation is not good for either of us.

She sits down on the hard surface beneath me, yawning.

"Take off your clothes," I say, unsure of how she will react.

"What?" she asks, her eyes bulging out of her head.

I continue to see my breath as I speak. "Body heat, it's what we need right now."

She rolls her eyes. "You just want to see me naked."

It wouldn't be the first time. I stifle a chuckle. "I'm not denying that, but I'm more concerned with making it out of this alive, and without hypothermia."

She glares at me before ripping her sweatshirt off. She shrieks loudly from the cold temperature outside. As she continues to remove her clothing, she eyes me down. "Well?"

I snort and then follow suit, ripping my own clothes from my body as quickly as possible.

She gets to her underwear and stops. "I think this is enough."

I glance over at her and take in her delicate body, her moderate chest, and her toned stomach. She has more ink than I remember from the last time I saw her like this, and they are all pretty big pieces. "Wow, you're more badass than I thought," I joke.

"Oh shut up." She rolls her eyes once more. "How do you want to do this?"

I take both of our sweatshirts and lay them on the cold, hard surface as a barrier before I grab her hands and lead her down with me. "Lay down," I instruct her, as I follow suit, spooning her. I place the blanket on top of us, snuggling as close as possible and keeping the ends pinned underneath our bodies. It's still colder than hell, but with my chest pressed up against her back, and my arms wrapped around her waist, I am finally understanding just how powerful body heat actually is.

Although we are slowly warming up, sleep is still a difficult task for us. The snow has ceased falling, but the sharp winds are rough.

I pull my head back slightly, admiring the circular tattoo she has between her shoulder blades. It is the size of a small Frisbee, and it's a Phoenix rising from the ashes. The red and black coloring to it makes it that much more intense. My thumb is trailing it before I can stop myself. Her body shudders beneath my touch, and as much as I'd like to think it's simply that, I know it's because of the circumstances, and because I am not pressed up against her. I pull her in tighter, squeezing her close.

"What do you think is going to happen?" she asks softly.

"What do I think is going to happen with what?" I attempt to understand her question.

"What do you think is going to happen with the cure?"

I can feel myself shrugging before I realize she can't see me. "I don't know. Do we even fully understand how it works yet?"

She shakes her head back and forth, her long hair rubbing against my chin. "I'm not even sure Jean-Luc knows. It obviously works while the host is still alive, but what about after?"

I breathe in deeply. "I'm not sure how it could. I mean, aren't they technically deceased by that point?"

She sighs. "That's what I was afraid of."

"What's on your mind, love?" I ask as I nuzzle my face into the back of her hair.

"I was thinking of Harlan, and how unfair all of this is."

I swallow, pulling away slightly. I hadn't expected her to bring Harlan up. I know she feels guilty for what happened to him, but for some reason, I thought she had moved past it.

Phoenix notices the distance, and ends up shifting her body so she is now facing me. The blanket slides off her shoulder and I quickly adjust it so she is still covered. She is shaking and I wrap my arms around her tightly, pulling her into my chest.

"You're stupid if you ever thought he stood a chance against you," she says barely above a whisper into the crook of my neck.

I release her enough that I can now look her in the eyes. "Excuse me?"

She surprises me by leaning in and pressing her lips to mine eagerly. "It was always you," she murmurs in between kisses.

I am kissing her back just as aggressively as she

is kissing me. Pretty soon our hands are touching and exploring each other's bare skin. The weather hasn't improved, but the blood rushing to my dick tells me I'm warming up quite nicely.

She pulls away from me, gasping for air. "So, tell me, Cullen, do you have anyone left?"

A sadness falls upon me. We are both orphans, but we have each other. "I'm looking at her."

Her facial expression turns solemn. "What happened to your aunt?"

I inhale sharply. My aunt has never been an easy subject for me. "She died from ovarian cancer while I was overseas."

She pulls even further away from me, shaking, but looking me deeply in the eyes. "I'm so sorry."

I shrug. "It was a long time coming. She got sick shortly after I graduated high school, and she was in and out of remission for years before it eventually claimed her."

She snuggles in closer, her nose in the crook of my neck. "You are such a strong person," I hear her say, as her warm breath tickles my neck.

I've had all the time in the world to feel sorry for myself, my life, and the circumstances. I don't need to dwell on the past. Being alone sucked, but over the years, I learned how to focus on what was important. Being in the military wasn't the easiest job in the world, it was rather lonely, but I was able to fill my time with women who made me feel something, even for a moment. It was my coping mechanism, and I was quite good at it...but Phoenix has continued to surprise and amaze me. No other woman has been able to captivate my attention so wholeheartedly. I can admit I haven't always been an upmost gentleman, but I want nothing more than to give Phoenix exactly what she deserves in life; someone who loves her and accepts all of her flaws.

I kiss the top of her head. "You're the strongest person I know."

She smiles solemnly before cuddling closer into my chest. I feel her yawn into my skin, and I know it's time for us to get some sleep. Once her breathing evens out and I'm positive she's asleep, I pull the blanket tighter around us.

She looks so peaceful, and even though I know she is heartbroken from losing Rian, she has a serene look upon her face. I graze her cheek softly with my finger, moving it from her cheekbone to her bottom lip. A few loose strands of hair have fallen upon her face, and I gently tuck them behind her ear.

I have no idea how she is so strong. I lost my parents when I was just a boy. I had years to grieve their deaths and move on. Even with my aunt, I had years to process the loss that was to inevitably come, and years to heal myself. She's lost her entire family in the matter of a couple of months, it has to be difficult. She never ceases to amaze me with her strength and beauty. Losing Rian was devastating for her, but I like to think I've done a decent job of keeping her mind occupied. She really hasn't had adequate time to grieve, but I know there is going to come a time when she will have to face it. As challenging as it will be when the time comes, I believe in her. I know she can overcome it.

"I don't know what it is about you, but you're feisty as hell, independent, and you always keep me guessing and on my toes. There's a million reasons why I don't deserve you, but now that I have you, I don't ever want to let you go," I whisper into her ear before closing my own eyes and giving in to the exhaustion.

* * *

A foot nudges me awake, and I open my eyes with a jolt. A fully dressed Phoenix is looking down at me, her arms crossed in front of her body. "Thank God, I thought I might have to inflict bodily harm to wake you up."

I squint my eyes, my blurry vision attempting to correct itself. "How long have I been out for?"

She shrugs. "Enough time for me to make this." She pulls out what appears to be a handmade slingshot from her pocket. It's nothing more than a pair of chopsticks, and a few rubber bands, but I'm surprised.

"Where did you get that?" I ask as I slowly stand.

"Whoa! Put that away before you hurt someone!" Phoenix cries, turning her back to me, and shielding her eyes.

At first I don't understand what she is referring to until I feel it. My eyes travel down my body, and sure enough, I'm sporting one hell of a case of morning wood.

"Oh, shite!" I curse, twirling around myself.

It's still freezing outside and I'm positive I won't have the problem much longer. Quickly,

I grab my clothes and begin slipping back into them. "It's nothing you haven't seen before," I tease her.

I hear her inhale sharply. "I wasn't in the right mind then."

I chuckle as I continue getting dressed.

"Is it safe to turn around?" Phoenix asks, just as I've zipped up my pants.

"Aye," I say, channeling my inner Scot.

She spins back around, her eyes trailing over my now clothed body. She is obviously flustered because her cheeks are a rosy color. I've never thought of Phoenix as shy, but I kind of enjoy this new side of her.

"I found this stuff in the storage closet downstairs yesterday. I wasn't really sure all of what I grabbed. But, pretty cool, right?" she answers my question finally.

"Well, have you tested it out yet?" I take a few steps toward her and reach for it, examining her work.

She nods. "Been trying it out all morning while you've been passed out."

"What have you been using?"

Her eyebrows raise with excitement. "Come here, look what I found." She begins walking to the opposite side of the roof, and I follow.

There is a pile of gravel just sitting in the corner amidst the snow. It's suspicious, but I'm excited she figured this out. "So, how does it work?"

She tosses her hair back as she speaks. "Well, I'm not the best shot, but I've been lucky a few times. I think it's a combination of the perfect shot and the right stone."

"Mind if I give it a go?" I ask as I lean down to choose the perfect stone.

She shakes her head. "Go right ahead."

I take a quick peek over the ledge, and then my eyes dart back to Phoenix. "Where did they all go?" I'm referring to the unusual absence of the biters from the night before. There are a few stragglers, but for the most part, they've moved on.

She shrugs. "It was like this when I woke up."

"Well we shouldn't waste any more time. Let's get off this bloody roof." I drop the stone and hand her back the slingshot, slipping the blanket back into my backpack and zipping it. I throw it on quickly before jogging over to the ladder and picking it up. We are off the roof in less than five minutes. We end up on foot for another several miles before we come to a red jeep. I'm thankful, I can barely concentrate on anything other than the blasted cold and the sick feeling in the pit of my stomach. We need food.

We climb into the jeep and lock the doors behind us. Phoenix climbs over the seats to the back to make sure we have no surprises before I begin searching for any sign of the keys. I know the odds are not in my favor, so when they drop from the overhead visor when I open it, I say a quick mental thank you to whatever higher power had a hand in that. My eyes trail over the gas gauge, and I'm happy to see we have a little more than half a tank.

"I could really go for some chicken and waffles right now," I joke.

Phoenix glances back at me curiously. "Are you sure you weren't raised in the south?"

I chuckle as I start the engine. "Positive. I'm just starving."

She nods. "Me too. Find us some food, will

you?"

I grin back at her as I pull out of the driveway. "Already on it, darling."

Thirteen – A Debilitating Attack

Ike

The shouting and screaming shakes me awake. At first I'm not sure if I am dreaming, hallucinating, or if the loud noises I am hearing are real. My eyes fly open and attempt to adjust to my surroundings. I can hear feet pounding on pavement and sounds of terror. My heart begins beating ferociously as I jump up from the cot, and make my way outside of my cell. People are running in every direction hysterically. I stop a young male teenager with brown hair. "What's going on?"

His eyes are large and frantic. "We're being attacked."

My heart falls to the pit of my stomach as I race all the way to the other side of the prison. I am headed to the area where the majority of the firearms are held. Pauly is nowhere in sight, but I do spot Brant handing out rifles and shotguns to a group of people lined up. I bypass the line and head straight for him. "What's going on?"

Brant continues handing out the weapons as he answers my question. "There's at least a hundred of them."

"Who?" I ask, glancing toward the barred windows.

"Degenerates. They showed up this morning demanding we give up *the* girl. When we told them we didn't know what they were talking about, they began advancing with their weapons drawn. We've been able to keep them outside of the gates, but now they've opened fire. I'm not sure how much longer the gate will be able to hold."

I grab one of the rifles from him swiftly, my blood boiling.

He reaches out for my arm, stopping me. "Please tell me this doesn't have to do with that girl you brought back here."

I breathe in deeply.

His brown eyes narrow. "Where is she, Ike?"

I sigh. "Even if I knew, I'd never give her up."

"Then you're stupid because you're putting everyone's lives at risk for one girl. What's so special about her anyway?"

When I don't answer, he seems to come to the

conclusion himself. "Oh my God. She's immune, isn't she?"

I clear my throat obnoxiously. "It'd be in your best interest to keep that bit of information to yourself. We already have enough to deal with as it is."

The sound of rapid gunfire continues outside, and I can't stand around talking any longer. Hastily, I make my way through the halls to the front of the prison. There are multiple people hiding behind the walls and popping out to shoot every now and again. I slide down the wall next to a middle-aged man with a gun. "What does it look like out there?"

He glances at me with wild eyes. "It's utter chaos."

"How many fatalities?"

His eyes look solemn. "We've lost count."

I look to the left and there are multiple people carrying in our injured peers. People are crying, shouting, screaming. It's almost worse than any war I've ever experienced.

I'm just about to head outside to help, when I notice a small figure huddled in the corner, whimpering. Curiosity gets the better of me as

I advance toward the tiny body. *Neveah*.

I reach out my hand to touch the young girl's knee. "Neveah, where's your mother?"

She lifts her head up and her eyes are filled with tears, her cheeks stained pink. My stomach flops. Suddenly, the urgency I felt to help with the attack outside has quieted inside of me, and all I can think of is how to keep this poor girl safe. "Here, come with me." I reach for her hand and although hesitant, she slips her small hand into mine.

I lead her back through the prison to our sleeping quarters. The gunfire is resonating from the front of the building. This is the safest place for her to be right now.

I know at this point Carmen didn't make it, but I don't know the circumstances to how it ended for her. I feel sick to my stomach. My mind replaying our last encounter over and over again. "Want to tell me what happened?" I ask in a soothing tone.

Neveah sniffles, her breath staggering. "We were outside, and the people outside the gates started shooting. My mom died protecting me."

I don't know what to say. I was just getting to

know Carmen…I was just beginning to fall for her. Neveah is so young. She doesn't deserve this.

I stay with Neveah until the sun goes down and the halls turn dark. The noises eventually stop, and I know the Degenerates have retreated for the night. It doesn't mean they won't be back. Neveah cries herself to sleep before I slip out, and head toward the destruction. Although it's temporarily over, the chaos continues. There are more than thirty injured and Jean-Luc is running around, attempting to get to as many as he can. He's recruited a few other helpers, mainly women who he is shouting instructions to over the wails of agony from all the injured. It's a gruesome sight. My stomach is twisted in knots.

I open the front door and take hesitant steps outside. The flood lights are on, so I can make out all of the lifeless bodies that lie scattered across the prison yard. I lose count of how many there are. It seems never-ending. I spot Carmen's honey-colored hair, and make my way over to her body. Her eyes are open along with her mouth, with a look of sheer horror across her face. She has multiple gunshot wounds, but I can tell the one that killed her was the shot to the head. I breathe in a deep, shaky breath, tears threatening to spill out. How the hell did this happen? *Is this all our fault?*

I lean down, stroking Carmen's cold cheek gently. "I'm so sorry. I never meant for this to happen." I stifle a sob as I'm reminded that she was alive less than twelve hours ago. We were in the beginning stages of something good, something positive and it was ripped away from us. I know it's karma for what I did to my family, but I don't want to accept it. There were so many qualities Carmen possessed that reminded me of my wife. I never thought I could feel that way again, and then Carmen proved me wrong.

As I close her eyelids slowly, the noise outside the gates catches my attention. On a good day, the biters outside the gates can be counted on two hands. Tonight, the number appears to have quadrupled due to all the commotion from earlier. They are all pressing on the fence, and because of the ruckus from before, I know there is not a chance in hell the gate will hold much longer. I stumble up quickly and make my way back inside, securing the door behind me. I hope Phoenix and Cullen are having better luck than we are here.

Fourteen – Playing House

Phoenix

We're within an hour of our destination, but the sun is going down and our fuel is running low so we decide to find a place to stay for the night. The Victorian-style home calls to me before we have a chance to pass it by. "Here." I point with my finger to the blue and white house.

Cullen pulls into the driveway, killing the engine. "Looks cozy," he says simply as he reaches into the backseat to grab his knife and the bag we've been carrying the antiserum in, tossing it over his shoulder. We both exit the vehicle, and my eyes dart all over our surroundings. I stay close to him as he reaches for the door handle, and neither one of us are surprised when it isn't locked.

Because of the amount of biters outside, we decide against turning on any lights. We know it will attract the wrong kind of attention, so we have our work cut out for us. "Stay here," Cullen orders me as I watch him leave the room, and I know he is looking for some sort of alternate light source. I've never been one to be babied, so I do the exact opposite and head down the hallway, my knife raised.

There are small bits of light shining through the windows in each of the rooms, making it easier than I thought to maneuver through the quaint house. My reflection in a closet mirror sends a shriek out of my mouth before I can stop it, and I hear something drop to the floor with a thud down the hallway, and footsteps running in my direction. My heart is just beginning to level out when Cullen pops his head in wide-eyed. "What the hell did I tell you?"

I shrug. "I'm not helpless."

"You might not be, but you're going to get yourself killed," he scolds.

"I'm not stupid either." I push angrily past him and make my way into the kitchen. I begin opening drawers quickly and sure enough, within moments, I find a couple of candlesticks, candles, and even a box of matches.

I give him a know-it-all smirk as I place the candles into their respective places and light them. It's a gold candlestick that reminds me of Beauty and the Beast. As we walk down the hallway, the wood creaks beneath us letting us know about the age of the house. I allow Cullen to lead the way up the stairs, as I light our path.

Once it's clear we are alone in the house, we lock all the doors and windows to make sure no one will be joining us, closing all the blinds. We raid the cupboards and fridge, but pass on the spoiled food we find. The cupboards are unusually stocked. It's surprising to think no one has bothered to come through the house before us today.

"Looks like it's our lucky day," Cullen says over his shoulder. "Pick your poison."

I end up choosing a can of peaches and a can of Ravioli by Chef Boyardee. Food has never tasted better. I savor every bite and even go as far as to drink the juice in the bottom of the peach can. It's sweet and quenches my thirst. Cullen opts for two cans of Spaghettios which he basically inhales in the matter of a few minutes after warming them on the stove. If I timed him, I'd bet he finished it in less than five minutes.

With our appetites fully satisfied, we make our way back upstairs to the bedrooms, and I end up claiming the first one, while Cullen chooses another one down the hall. Although I am beyond the realm of exhaustion, insomnia takes hold of me. I miss Rian with every fiber of my being. I want to scream, punch, and kick anything in sight. The pillow underneath me takes a massive beating between my fist and my tears. *I couldn't protect her...*

I end up drawing myself a hot bath and soaking it until my mind shuts off and my skin becomes wrinkly. I'd forgotten what it feels like to enjoy the simple things such as soaking in a tub. Once I finish, I make my way back to the bedroom I claimed and lie down back in the bed. My body feels exhausted, but my mind has another agenda altogether. I keep picturing Rian's face right before they slit her throat, the blood seeping down her body. Rage is once again taking hold of me and I'm sobbing and punching the pillow beside me. *It's all my fault.*

After tossing and turning for what feels like an agonizing couple of hours, I finally give up the fight, and end up making my way into the room Cullen chose. Shadows play upon the walls and floor as I tiptoe into the room, and then crawl under the covers beneath him. I close my eyes once again hoping the change of scenery will help.

I feel his hand reach out, grazing over my thigh, and I turn over so I am on my side facing him. "I'm sorry if I woke you up."

He shrugs. "I've been awake for a while. I was having trouble sleeping through all the commotion from your room."

My cheeks instantly begin burning up. *I wasn't aware you could hear me.* I mean, don't get me wrong, I definitely wasn't quiet, but I didn't take into consideration the fact that he may have been listening in to everything.

"You okay?" he asks gently.

"What kind of a question is that?" I retort snidely.

He cradles my face with his hand before swiping his finger across my warm cheek. My tears have long since dried, but my emotions are still at an all-time high. "I care about you, Phoenix. I'm just trying to be here for you."

I'm not used to being vulnerable to anyone. Vulnerability means weakness. Yet somehow, in this exact moment, it's the thing I want most in the world. I find myself leaning into his caress, closing my eyes.

I press my lips to his quickly, before I maneuver myself so that I am sitting on him. Even in the darkness I can see his eyes widen from my movement. "What are you doing?" he asks.

"Shhh…" I press my finger to his lips. "I'm

trying to forget."

I lean down, pressing my lips gently to his neck and I hear him release a labored breath. I continue pressing kisses down his neck, toward his collarbone. Each kiss solicits an extreme response from him, and I find myself surprised at how excited the simple touch is making him.

He sits up so we are level; I'm still situated on his lap, and then he presses his lips to mine eagerly, moaning in my mouth. I feel his arms circle my back and then suddenly, he's managed to trade places with me. I find myself flat on my back, and Cullen lowers his body down on top of mine. I can feel the excitement from under his pants, and my heart begins to ricochet off my ribcage.

Roughly, he throws my hands above my head, pinning them to the headboard as his mouth explores my exposed skin. His touch feels like heaven, and I want nothing more than for him to rip my clothes off and take all of me.

He continues to keep me pinned down as he lowers his lips to my ear. "You have no idea how long I've been waiting for this moment."

If I were a guy, I'd have pre-cummed right then and there. "So do it."

His grip on my wrists tightens, and I think he is going to tell me something else, when I feel him bite down on my earlobe. It's not gentle. It's animalistic.

I open my mouth to say something else when he shushes me again. "You have no idea how badly I want this right now, how badly I want you, but...I can't."

His words surprise me. I tilt my head to the side, locking eyes with him. "Why not?"

"It's not the right time. We both know this."

I shake my head dismissively, then pull my wrists out of his grasp. "I'm underneath you. I'd say now is as good of time as any."

Cullen rolls off me slowly and onto his back beside me. "That's not what I mean, and you know it."

"You're a guy!" I cry out, throwing my arms up in exasperation. "You can't tell me you don't want this."

He sighs loudly. "Oh, I want it."

"Then what's the problem?" I push, turning my face toward him.

"When I fuck you it's not going to be because I'm trying to make you feel better. And it sure as hell isn't going to be because I want to get off. It's going to be because I'm hopelessly in love with you, and I want to show you how much by making love to you."

His words leave me breathless. I've never been spoken to this way before. My respect for him grows. He is being a true gentleman. Sex tonight would just be a distraction for me, and that's not what I want either. I want to be fully present when he rips me apart and puts me back together again.

Fifteen – Trapped

Cullen

We get a head start on the day, leaving as soon as the sun rises. When we are within miles of the White House, I pull the car off to the side of the road.

"What are you doing?" Phoenix asks, eyeing me curiously.

"We have no idea what we are walking into, and given our past track record, I'd say it'd be in our best interest to have some sort of leverage," I respond, unbuckling and grabbing the backpack filled with the antiserum.

I unzip the bag, reaching into it, grabbing out a handful of the vials, no more than six. "I think we need a back-up stash, just in case."

Phoenix looks from me to the vials. "You're probably right."

I nod, handing her back the lighter bag. "Stay here. I'll be right back." I know this is probably going to irritate her more than anything, because Phoenix hates to be viewed as weak. I exit the car swiftly, holding the vials close to my chest. There are a few biters roaming the street, and some take note of me, but not too many to make me nervous.

I quickly make my way down the street and around a corner. I find a big shrub and drop my handful of vials down in the middle of it, making sure they aren't obvious to the eye. Then, I take out my knife and cut a small piece of my shirt off, and attach it to one of the small branches. It's the only thing I can think of to mark it.

My ears perk up as the sound of dragging feet hones in. I lift my eyes, and sure enough there is a ghoulish looking biter headed straight for me. His eyes are sunken in with black circles around them, and he is so skinny, his ribs are visibly pushing against his thin layer of skin. He has no clothes on but a worn pair of shorts and what appears to be one flip-flop. The skin has deteriorated around his mouth and nose, and his eyes are glossy and bloodshot.

He seems to have brought friends. My eyes notice movement behind him as two more biters slowly approach me. I really miss having a gun, even though the loud noise usually isn't to our benefit. I even miss the baseball bats Ike used to carry around. Having just a small knife elicits twice the work to put a biter down without being bitten. The biter closest to me lunges at me, and I manage to dodge him just in time. I spin around, bringing the knife down into his skull with force. He goes limp. I rip the knife out of his skull as quickly as I can, before I take on the other two.

Once my imminent threats are out of the way, I make my way back to our vehicle and notice Phoenix is outside of the car, with a pile of biters lying at her feet. There is black blood oozing down the street, coming straight toward me.

"You just couldn't stay put, could you?" I ask as I watch her take her knife to a biters eye, subduing her.

She glances back at me. "Now, what would be the fun in that?"

I grin, opening the door and climbing back in. She follows suit. "Where did you put them?"

I turn the key, starting the engine. "Somewhere safe."

I can see her roll her eyes out of the corner of mine.

"So, what is our plan?" she asks as we drive toward our destination.

I shrug. "I'm not sure what we are going to find when we get there. But, until we know it's safe, let's only mention the fact that we have found a cure, not the fact that we have multiples."

She nods. "It's probably smart then to keep the fact that I'm immune between the two of us."

The huge white building comes into focus along with the long black gate surrounding the property. There are biters all along the fence, reaching their arms out to nothing in particular. I slow the car to a crawl as we near the President's home. We do a full circle of the property, taking note of the heavily guarded entrance. There appears to be military soldiers all dressed in black.

"How many do you think there are?" Phoenix asks in a near whisper.

I blow out a long breath of air. "More than twenty, that's for sure." The soldiers are secure within the confines of the gate, and each one holds up a black, sleek rifle. The shots ring out loud and clear, attracting more biters no doubt.

"There's no way they will allow us to keep our weapons," Phoenix says in a stressed tone.

I raise my eyebrow. "Then we take a leap of faith and trust that they are who they say they are."

She groans.

"Are you ready for this?" I ask her as I pull up to the entrance. I can feel the eyes on our vehicle.

She takes a deep breath. "Let's go save the world."

We tuck our knives for safe-keeping, and then exit the vehicle. I am carrying the bag filled with the antiserum over my shoulder.

"Stop right there! Don't move!" A powerful voice booms loudly.

I exchange a wary glance with Phoenix before we both raise our hands in surrender. "Listen, we just want to talk, calmly."

A man with grey hair and blue eyes steps forward. He is stocky and dressed differently than the rest of the soldiers. He has a white goatee and is wearing what I can only assume to be one hell of an expensive suit. His dark blue tie enhances his eyes. "Who are you?" he asks.

"My name is Ace Cullen and this is Phoenix, we are looking to speak with the President."

The stocky gentleman laughs heartily. "Sure you are. That's what they all say. What makes you think we would let you anywhere near him?"

I can feel Phoenix's eyes on me as I unzip the bag and reach into it. The air grows thick with tension as all the guns lock on me. "Because, I come bearing a cure."

His blue eyes widen as I hear whispers throughout the small army.

"You have my attention," he says.

Guns begin to go off in a chorus of fire and I fall to my feet, crouching, protecting my head. I look to my right and Phoenix hasn't missed a beat. When my mind registers the fact that we are both unharmed, I swivel my head behind us and notice four biters lifeless on the ground.

I stand back up, irritated they didn't have the common courtesy to tell us to duck.

"Who are you?" I ask, eyeing each of the soldiers. They are wearing helmets with plastic face covers.

"I am George Nagel, Secretary of Defense, and this is the 41st Infantry Brigade."

His answer satisfies me. "I'm from the 38th Infantry Brigade myself."

George's eyebrows raise. "Well, why didn't you say so? Open the gates," he shouts behind him.

More gunshots go off mere inches from our faces as we enter the property, slowly.

"We're going to have to confiscate any weapons you might have. I hope you understand. Can't have the President in any harm," he says in a gentle voice.

Phoenix gives me a know-it-all look before pulling her knife out from behind her back, and slowly placing it on the ground. I do the same with my own knife.

"We are going to need to search you, for assurance of course," George says.

We both nod stiffly. "Of course," I reply.

As we are both patted down, George unzips my bag, reaching into it and pulling out a few of the vials. He eyes them, rolling them between his fingers. "If you don't mind me asking, how in the world did you manage to get your hands on these?"

I exchange a wary glance with Phoenix before

she speaks up. "We knew someone who was immune and we know a doctor."

"You speak in past tense. What happened to them?" he asks.

"She died." Phoenix responds matter-of-factly, and I know then she is trying to play it off as if Rian was the immune donor.

"I'm sorry to hear that," George replies, placing the antiserum back into the bag, and then handing it back to me.

"Follow me," he orders as the soldiers part and make a pathway for us. Half of them remain guarding the fence and the other half follows behind us, their guns held protectively in front of them. I watch as they march, noticing that they are not in sync, not even close. It's a small observation, but it's enough to make me uneasy. Soldiers are trained very specifically in the Army, the National Guard, and even the Reserves. Something feels off. I suddenly feel very naked without my knife.

We are led inside the enormous building. Large chandeliers hang from the ceiling, red and gold curtains adorn the windows, and it's apparent the building has had its necessary upkeep.

George stops walking abruptly, turning to face

both Phoenix and me. "Unfortunately, we can only take one of you in to meet the President," George says, and I can tell he's already made up his mind as to which one of us will get the liberty. "Cullen, if you can follow me, I'll lead the way."

Phoenix's eyes widen as she locks them with mine. It's a silent plea. She doesn't think splitting up is a good idea. *Well darling, neither do I.* But the soldiers holding the rifles tell me that we don't have much of a choice. I reach my hand up to her face, caressing it gently. "It's going to be okay. I'll try not to take too long."

She nods stiffly, her cheek rubbing back and forth against my palm. I lean in, pressing my lips close to her ear. "If they give you any reason to believe they are not who we think, don't hesitate. Give 'em hell."

She nods, silently. I press my lips gently to the top of her head before following George down the hall. The soldiers split up once more, seven staying back with Phoenix. It's a long walk to the Oval Office, and I'm surprised by how quiet it is. Before the infection, the White House was known to house hundreds of people a day inside these walls. Now, it seems eerie and still.

We finally approach the door and George

opens it, peeking his head in. "President, sir, you have a visitor." He steps back out into the hall, and motions for me to enter. The soldiers don't follow this time. As I enter the Oval Office, the door shuts behind me, and the guards along with George remain on the other side of the door.

The famous desk sits in front of me with the infamous Presidential seal underneath it. The black chair is turned facing the opposite direction of me, and I take a few hesitant steps into the room. "Mr. President?"

"Take a seat," I hear from behind the chair. I do as I am told, making my way to the striped red and white couches in the middle of the room. The first thing I take notice of are the bright lights on the ceiling, shining down on us. My eyes spy a camera off to the side of the left wall, and I swivel around noticing an identical one off to the right wall. They are watching my every move. My eyes wander more around the large room, and land on a suspicious red stain on the adjacent wall. My stomach dips as my eyes scan my surroundings more thoroughly. In each corner of the room, closest to the door, I notice the greyed bodies of what I can only deduce as biters. They have no arms and wear similar headgear as the soldiers that stand outside the door. Both have a metal collar similar to a canines, and they are connected to a metal chain which are attached to the walls.

I hear the creak of the chair turning around, and my eyes lower as an unfamiliar muscular male locks eyes with me. President Jackson is in his fifties, with grey hair and a bit of a belly. The gentleman seated behind his desk looks Cuban and no older than forty. I swallow my fear down. *God I hope Phoenix is alright.*

Sixteen – A New Form of Control

Phoenix

As I watch Cullen and a handful of guards walk away from me, something feels amiss. I understand being overly cautious and protective of the leader of our nation, but to split us up after we came bearing such a huge gift, seems odd.

"Miss, please follow us," one of the soldiers turns to address me.

"Excuse me?" I ask, my eyes instantly shooting back up at the sound of a door closing down the long hallway.

"We'd like to show you to the formal waiting room," the soldier replies, wrapping his fingers around my arm.

I attempt to pull my arm from his grasp, but his fingers only tighten. "I'm fine waiting here."

His hold on my arm does not lessen. "We will bring him to you when he's finished."

I sigh loudly. I have no choice. I'm surrounded by a handful of soldiers, all whom are heavily armed compared to myself. I have to do as I am told.

As they begin leading me the opposite way that I watched Cullen go, I feel the need to get some answers. "I don't understand why I am not allowed to meet the President as well."

The soldier still has a grip on my arm and stops walking abruptly, turning to face me. I can see his brown eyes underneath his plastic faceguard and they don't look kind. "Unarmed or not, you can still be a threat to the President. We try to keep his visits to a minimum to avoid that."

Before I have a chance to respond, I am being pulled into an elevator. My heart begins beating out of my chest as I realize that wherever we are going is not on the same level as Cullen.

My eyes trail about the top of the metal box, noticing a small camera pointed at us in the corner. *I wonder who is watching.*

When the door opens on the bottom level, it's obvious we are in the basement. Concrete walls and floors are covering the lower level. My heart rate begins to steadily increase because I can't imagine this to be the formal waiting room. My eyes travel around the eerie basement, trying to pay attention to every little detail. It could be my only shot between life and death.

As we get deeper into the cold basement, my stomach drops when the sounds of moans and wails enter my ears. There are metal cages housed with hundreds of people. The people look dirty, they look hungry, but most of all, they look unstable. They are all reaching through the metal bars, attempting to grab us as we walk by.

"What the hell is this?" I ask angrily, my eyes growing wider by the minute.

"Welcome to your new home," the soldier answers who's been dragging me along. His grip releases on my arm, and my one and only thought is to run. I duck beneath their arms and bodies as I try to make my escape, but I'm stopped when multiple arms and hands grab ahold of my body. I'm thrown roughly to the ground; the wind knocked out of me. I'm gasping, attempting to catch my breath when a series of large hands pin me down to the cold, hard concrete floor. I watch helplessly as one of the soldiers pushes up the sleeve of my hoodie, and removes a lid to a syringe, the long needle piercing the skin in my arm. I feel something large and uncomfortable being shot into my arm before they pull me up from the ground roughly and shove me into one of the cages, along with all the others. The eyes surrounding me look desperate, yet tired.

The people in the cages are wearing expensive clothing and if it weren't for their unusually dirty state, I'd guess they were all influential beings before the infection spread. A woman in the corner appears to be more put together than the rest. Her hair appears only slightly greasy, and her clothes aren't nearly as worn as the others. She has kind eyes and soft features. There is empathy behind her eyes.

"Hello," I say tentatively, taking a few hesitant steps toward her, attempting to show her I'm not a threat.

Her mouth curves into a small smile. "Hello."

"What is going on here?" I ask, my eyes shifting around nervously. "Who are all these people?"

She blinks a few times. "The White House staff, Secret Service..." she trails off.

Now it is beginning to make sense why they are dressed as they are. The soldiers who brought me down here are out of place. Who knows if they are even part of the military?

"What did they do to me?" I ask, eyeing my now bruised arm.

The kind woman reaches out for my arm, running her finger across my bruise lightly. "They installed a tracker."

My eyes widen. A tracker? "What the hell do they plan to do with that?" I ask nervously, my thoughts running wild.

She shrugs slightly before releasing my arms.

My eyes spot an older gentleman in the corner of the metal cage and I do a double-take. *No way.* Either my eyes are deceiving me, or I am staring directly at the President of the United States. My situation only seems to get worse. I have no idea where they took Cullen or who he is with, but I now know without a fraction of a doubt, it can't be good.

* * *

Cullen

"Who the hell are you?" I ask shortly, as I stand up and back away from the desk.

The unfamiliar man stands, straightening his suit jacket, before taking a few steps toward me. "What's the matter?" he asks in a condescending tone. "Were you expecting someone else?"

The temperature in my body rises as my eyes dart around the room.

"I'm the leader of this great nation of ours," he says with authority. "And you are?"

"The hell you are!" My voice comes out louder than I intend. "What the hell did you do to President Jackson?" My eyes wander back over to the wall, where the red stain is now taunting me. I fear the worst.

"President Jackson isn't in charge any more. I am." He closes even more distance between us. "You can call me President Cruz. I hear you managed to get your hands on an antiserum. Is that correct, Mr.—?" He waits for me to fill in the blank.

"Cullen," I snap.

"Cullen. What an interesting name. British, I presume?" I'm not sure why it matters to him, but I decide to humor him anyway by nodding.

"I figured as much from your accent." He has an accent himself, but it's faint.

"May I?" He reaches his hand out for my bag

and I pull away quickly, before I can stop myself.

He pulls his hand back, smiling. "It would be in your best interest to be cooperative, Cullen. I don't want to have a reason to call my men in here to force you to comply."

I would rather not have to deal with a handful of rifles aimed at my head either, so I give in. I slowly hand him the bag.

He unzips it and pulls out one of the vials, inspecting it closely. "Where did you get this?"

My eyes shift to the door before landing back on his face. "I have nothing else to say unless you bring Phoenix in here."

He raises his eyebrows. "Phoenix?"

"The girl I was traveling with. Your men made her wait in the hall."

He nods stiffly. "Another unique name." He places the vial back in the bag before setting it on the couch beside him. "Very well then. Guards!"

The door opens and three soldiers race in, gripping their rifles tightly. I watch as he whispers something to the first guard. The soldier nods with understanding before they begin to make their way back out the door. One of the soldiers stops directly in front of me and slams the butt of his rifle into my face. I fall backwards, throwing my hand over my now gushing nose. "What the hell?"

"I want you to understand who is in charge here, Cullen. It seems as though you needed a little reminder," Cruz says twirling the ring on his finger around and around.

Blood is dripping out of my nose onto the no longer pristine carpet. I contemplate making a run for it, but the rifles they carry tell me I won't make it far.

"Get a towel to clean that mess up," Cruz orders the soldier.

I watch as the soldier leaves the room and we are yet again, alone.

"Listen, I don't want to hurt you. Really, I don't. But, in order to guarantee that, you are going to need to talk."

I don't want to be cooperative in the least, but I have no idea if Phoenix is okay and if I am the cause of harm to her, I'll never forgive myself. "There is a doctor back in Tennessee who manufactured it."

Cruz nods his head slowly as he leans back against the large, mahogany desk. "Who was the blood donor?"

"There was a girl—Rian, but she was killed. A shot to the head."

"Now that's a pity, isn't it?" Cruz replies, as the soldier returns with a wet towel and begins attempting to get the blood out of the carpet. They don't bother offering me anything to clean myself up with. Blood is now dripping down my face and onto my sweatshirt. "Now, you wouldn't happen to be lying to me about her death, would you?" Cruz takes a few steps toward me, staring me down intently.

No. But I am lying to you about the real donor.

"No," I reply through gritted teeth.

"Very well." He begins pacing about the room. "Let's test it out, shall we?"

My heart begins to beat ferociously against my ribcage. I have no idea what the bastard has in store for me now.

"Let's go," Cruz orders me as he begins making his way toward the door.

"Where are you taking me?" I ask hesitantly,

not moving a muscle.

He looks back at me. "If what you say is true, and this antiserum actually works, then I've become even more powerful than ever. This will enable us the opportunity to trade the cure for more guns, ammo, and even food."

My eyes narrow. "Eventually, you are going to run out...what then?" He crosses the room to me and I'm not sure what to expect. He begins pulling up his pant leg and my eyes travel to the skin exposed. There is a huge scar across the length of it. He drops his pant leg and then rolls his sleeve up showing me his forearm. "Are those..."

Cruz finishes my question for me. "Bite marks? They sure are."

"But how?" My mind begins racing.

"Your donor wasn't the only one immune to the infection. I am too. Once I realized the power I wielded, it wasn't difficult rising to the top. I'm like a God around these parts. They will protect me with their lives." I am left speechless.

"They've been trying to manufacture the cure for months with my blood. Unfortunately, all of our test subjects have died. You see, we've had almost every piece to the puzzle; my blood, a doctor…the only thing we've been missing is the correct combination of substances…until now. Fifty three unsuccessful trials to date. Fifty three dead hosts. It's time to put your word to the test." He turns away from me, walking toward the door. "Come along now, Cullen, you get a front row seat."

* * *

I am led into a room three levels below the Oval Office. The room is stark white and sterile looking. It smells strongly of bleach, and I know it's because of how many failed trials they've done. Bright fluorescent lights shine down from the ceiling and there is a doctor in a white jacket with his back turned to us when we enter. He is hovering over a body, holding a device up to his mouth.

"Time of death, 9:43 a.m." I hear the sound of a click and realize it is a recorder he is holding.

"President Cruz," the doctor turns around nervously. "What can I do for you?" The doctor is dark-skinned, with obscure brown eyes, and balding black hair. He looks Indian. He is short and stout.

It is apparent this doctor is intimidated by Cruz and his small army of soldiers. If I had to guess,

I'd say they've been holding him against his will. "Actually Dr. Kapur, I think the better question is, what can we do for you?"

Dr. Kapur's eyes widen, confused. Cruz motions for one of the soldiers to hand him the bag with the antiserum. Once he has it, he reaches in, and grabs one of the vials, handing it to the doctor. The doctor looks surprised, his eyes darting between all of us in the room. "Where did you get this?"

Cruz slaps his hand on my back. "Our new friend here. He claims it's a working cure."

The doctor's eyes train on me and I can tell he has many questions.

"I thought we could test it out." Just as the words leave his mouth I hear the gurgling sound from the deceased corpse and know a biter has just been born. It isn't seconds before one of the soldiers shoots the newbie biter in the head, putting him down for good.

"We're going to need a test subject," Dr. Kapur states.

"Already have that covered." Cruz shifts his attention to the soldiers standing guard at the door. "Bring him in."

The door opens and two soldiers drag a man in who appears to be unconscious. His head is down, but there is something familiar about him I can't put my finger on. He is just coming to when his head bobs up slowly, his eyes barely open. I know without a shadow of a doubt the identity of their newest test subject: *President Jackson*.

* * *

President Jackson is shouting and thrashing about the moment he comes to. The fear in his eyes and voice transfers over to me. "You can't do this!" he shouts. "I'm the President of the United States. I'll give you anything you want. Money? It's yours."

Cruz laughs in a sinister way. "Money? What good would that do for me now? I have everything I need."

The President's eyes widen from fear. "You won't get away with this!" I watch helplessly as they strap him down to a metal table, subduing his hands and feet.

I can't believe I am standing idly by while they secure the President of our nation. I glance back at the soldiers in the room, and my eyes trail over their rifles. I don't think there is going to be a way out of this. I feel like I have failed our leader—our country.

The doctor opens one of the vials of the antiserum, dipping the tip of a syringe in it and filling it slowly. I hear the creak of the door and look back to see another soldier leading in one of the armless biters I encountered earlier. It's still wearing a helmet, but as they near the President, the soldier reaches for it, removing it. The President begins screaming, begging for help and it makes me sick to my stomach. I can't watch. I turn around, averting my eyes.

One of the soldiers shoves me in the chest with the tip of his rifle, urging me to turn back around. I spin around just as the biter sinks his teeth into the President's arm. A rifle goes off immediately after, sending the biter to the floor, limply. His black blood is scattered across the walls, floor, and the President's face.

President Jackson is still hysterical, his cries now a mixture of fear and pain. Instead of immediately injecting him with the cure, the doctor insists on waiting for the infection to spread a bit more. I'm not sure how many minutes pass by as we simply observe the President in his changing state. First the more subtle changes take place: his breathing becomes labored, and his eyes gloss over, the veins expanding in size.

As the time ticks by, the President becomes more distraught and agitated. He isn't screaming anymore, instead now growling.

I watch as the doctor takes a sample of the antiserum, placing it on a glass slide and places it into a microscope. He leans down, taking a look at it. "Interesting," he mumbles to himself. "Very interesting."

"Can we move this along?" One of the soldiers asks irritated.

The doctor steps away from the microscope, grabbing the syringe and stepping closer to the President. We all watch as he injects the President slowly, and he stops thrashing. In fact, President Jackson becomes so still, the doctor leans in to see if he is still breathing. The air grows thin in the entire room. I feel like we all are holding our breath collectively, waiting to see the result. The President sucks in a large gasp, causing the doctor to jump back, startled. I can feel all the rifles trained directly on President Jackson, ready to take him out if the outcome is not favorable. The President takes a few more deep breaths before his breathing appears to return to normal.

Cruz turns toward me, his eyes dancing with joy. "I am going to be the most powerful man in the world."

The soldiers begin rejoicing along with him, and the sickness in my stomach only intensifies.

"Are you going to be able to recreate it?" Cruz addresses the doctor.

"Yes, but it is going to take a little bit of time," the doctor replies.

Cruz shrugs and then chuckles, slapping me on the shoulder. "We wouldn't have been able to do this without you." He shifts his eyes from me to the soldiers behind me. "Take him away."

My eyes grow wide. "What?" I choke out. "I just handed over the cure. You owe me!"

Cruz seems to contemplate this for a second. "You're right. He deserves the royal treatment. Throw him in cage two."

I feel fingers gripping my arms and I wrestle against them to no avail. *I am screwed.* I'm being dragged down a concrete hallway when I hear Phoenix's familiar voice. "Cullen?" she cries out as I pass by a series of cages, all filled with people. The soldiers stop in front of a cage that is different than the others. This one is filled with biters. The biters inside all resemble the ones from the Oval Office. They have no arms and are wearing headgear. All I can hear as they throw me inside are the loud cries coming from Phoenix.

Seventeen – Reveling in the Kill

Ike

Phoenix and Cullen have been gone for over seven days. Knowing that Washington is only ten hours away, I don't have the best feeling swirling inside of me about their mission. The prison is no longer safe and I can't sit idly by and wait for another attack from Degenerates, so I pack up as many supplies as I can in preparation to leave on foot with Jean-Luc and Neveah. Jean-Luc has done all he can for the many injured still left at the prison, and at this point, I need to protect him as he is the only person who knows how to manufacture the cure. There are only fifty people left alive at the prison and they've been looking to me for leadership and guidance. The military leaders we first met when we arrived are no longer alive. I know these people need me, but I need Cullen and Phoenix. I need to live.

I gather everyone in the lunch room of the prison, standing atop one of the tables to command attention. "My friends, it is no longer safe within the confines of these walls. I won't make the decision for you, but I will decide for myself. We are leaving for Washington. I don't know what we will be greeted with when we arrive, but it can't be anything worse than what we have been experiencing here. There is hope in Washington. There are still enough guns and ammo for half of us, and we can supplement with other weapons for the rest. You don't have to make the decision now, but we are leaving today." I pause, looking around the room at all the eyes trained on me. "We are leaving so that we can ensure a better future."

Audible whispers are coming from all over the mess hall. I know it's a big order, to take all of the survivors along with us, but I can't leave them here in good conscience. The majority of them are mothers and children. There are a few teenagers, but only one or two capable soldiers left. I know it is on my shoulders to protect them.

Although Washington is merely ten hours away, our group is much too big to make the journey in one day. To be able to locate enough vehicles for the lot of us will take ample time, not to mention the breaks we will have to take along the way. I guestimate we will arrive within three days. There are injured peers who will never make it out of the prison. I am not delusional and they are not either. To transport them in the state they are in would only be more of a detriment and hindrance for the entire group. I hate that we will have to leave them behind, but if we don't go now, the Degenerates will return and there is a possibility none of us would make it out alive.

I take the remaining soldiers and teenage boys, supplying them with the firearms. The mothers and children will be equipped with knives, tire irons, and whatever we can scrounge up. Although Jean-Luc isn't confident behind a gun, I supply him with one of the rifles as well. It's the least I can do to guarantee his survival.

There is one prison van left and lucky for us it has a full tank of gas and keys. We are able to fit nearly sixteen people into it. The rest of us take off on foot. It's midday when we make our way out of the prison and onto the main road. By my count, we are going to need more than six vehicles to make the trip. The first three vehicles come easily, and we fill them up as quickly as possible, locking the doors to each of them. In the third one, I send them off to scour for more vehicles. They return shortly after with another one.

More than half of our people are now secured inside the vehicles, equipped with food, water, and weapons, but the remainder are still on foot. Biters trail behind us at a distance, but it leaves me uneasy. One wrong move, and I could lose the people I am leading. Jean-Luc and Neveah are safe in one of the vehicles, so that puts some of my mind at ease. It's nearing nightfall by the time we locate the last two vehicles and begin caravanning down the Tennessee freeway. It is littered with biters, overturned cars and debris, but we make it through at a slower pace.

Just as we hit the state border, something catches my eye up ahead. I am driving the prison van, and I step on the brake when I see the roadblock. I know instantly that something isn't right, but we have been driving for hours now, and if we turn around and go back the opposite way, it will take double, if not triple the time to make it to Cullen and Phoenix. The roadblock is in front of us, at least a quarter of a mile away. "Stay here," I warn my passengers as I hastily climb out of the van, gripping my rifle. Within seconds, bullets are whizzing past my face and at the windshield of the van. "Duck!" I scream as loudly as possible. I spin back around, and begin releasing a round of bullets in the opposite direction, hoping to hit a few of our attackers.

I hear more bullets flying past my ears, but they are originating from behind me. I steal a quick glance and notice that half of my group are now in tow with me, fighting back. I hear shots ricocheting off the vehicles, hitting the metal, and cries of fear and pain emanating from all around me. I continue shooting, but out of the corner of my eye, I begin to see members of my group go down. I duck and then look back, my guilt already beginning to kick my ass. A handful of my group are on the ground, bleeding out. I know without any more doubt that we are up against Degenerates.

Rage takes over my body and motions, and I charge our attackers, without thinking clearly. I end up taking out three of them within a thirty second span. The shots coming at us have died down severely. As soon as I am within a few feet of them, I notice that there are only a handful of them left. I take out two more, narrowly missing bullets coming straight at me. That's when I see her. She exits one of their vehicles they are using as part of the roadblock, locks eyes with me, and then begins running the opposite direction.

What the hell?

I duck, narrowly missing a bullet to the head. *Degenerates.* This whole time, we've been under attack by Degenerates. *How the hell did they find us?*

My eyes follow Jerrica who is bolting off the freeway and into the side grass. *There's no way I'm letting you get away.*

I follow her lead, racing to catch up to her

when an arm comes out and strikes me directly in the gut. I keel over, attempting to catch my breath. "You just don't want to die, do you?" his trailer trash accent comes out and I look up. A disgusting Earl is staring back down at me. I stumble backwards, shoving my rifle into his face. "Oh, come on now, that's not a fair fight," Earl states, making it obvious that he is not equipped with a firearm.

I press the rifle closer to his face. "How did you find us?" I ask.

Earl chuckles, a wild look taking over his eyes. "Who says we were looking for you?"
My stomach drops. Could it be possible that they were simply laid out, waiting and ready to pull the same damn trick they've pulled on us time and time again on other unsuspecting victims, and we just so happened to walk right into it?

Earl capitalizes on my hesitation and charges at me. He's wrestling with me for control of the gun, when it goes off, a bullet striking him in the chest. He staggers backward, falling to the ground. I take a couple of steps toward Earl, standing over his body as the blood pools out from his wound. He is trying to talk, but no words are coming out. I point the rifle directly at his skull, pulling the trigger. The impact is so strong, his blood splatters up, hitting me in the face. The old Ike would have remorse for killing someone. I'm not that man anymore. I want each and every one of them to pay for what they did to Rian—what they did to Foster. I have no remorse left.

I hop over his body and fly off the main road, into the grass. I can still see Jerrica in the distance, but she has been slowed down by biters who heard all the commotion. She is surrounded by a group of five or so biters, and is taking them down one by one, but if I don't do something they are going to kill her. No one deserves that more than Phoenix. I close in on her and shoot all five dead within seconds. She spins around to see who has come to her rescue, then her face falls when she sees me. "Still have a soft spot for me, don't you, Ike?"

I keep the rifle trained on her, but look around assessing the incoming biters. They are far enough away to not stress about them just quite yet. "More like a thorn in my side," I reply sharply.

She rolls her eyes. "You and I both know you can't go through with this, so why don't you give up the charade and we can go our separate ways?" She begins to walk away, unaware that she doesn't know me as well as she'd like to believe.

"Yeah, you're probably right," I say. "At least not any more than you could go through with killing your children."

She stops walking abruptly, spinning around to face me. I'm not sure what I expected when she turned around, but the sickening smile she is beaming at me was definitely not it. She takes a step toward me. "What did they tell you?"

I swallow, realizing just how sick and twisted she is. "Enough."

She giggles. "I started with Jackson. I knew he was going to be the most difficult to pull off, so I knew I would have to do it while he was asleep. I remember the feeling of the knife between my fingertips as I cut open his throat, exposing his vocal chords."

Chills run up and down my spine similar to how they did the first time I heard the story.

She inches toward me. "He was perfect. He didn't even make a sound. I snuck into Josiah's room next. I never understood why my husband had that gun, much less a silencer...but it came in handy when I took the pillow to Josiah's face to muffle his screams as I shot him."

I back up as she continues to inch closer. I

don't want to hear anymore, but I haven't decided how I want to handle the situation quite yet.

"I went to Jerrad's room next. The little fucker woke up while I was sneaking in. I can still remember the lopsided grin he wore as I entered. He had *no* idea. The police report said I crushed his skull with the hammer, but who really knows. I just remember the hair and brains that stuck to the end of it."

Her words make me nauseous as I imagine her poor kid being bludgeoned to death. I throw my arm up across my mouth, dry heaving.

"Jillian must have heard me though, because when I went into her room, she wasn't in her bed. I went from room to room calling out her name sweetly, telling her I was looking for her, and the little bitch never came out. Would you believe the little cunt was hiding in her own closet? A thirteen year old girl, and she couldn't find a better hiding spot? I dragged her out by her hair. She was screaming so loudly, I was sure she was going to wake our neighbors. The screams only got louder when I stabbed her in the eye with her own pair of scissors." She giggles sadistically. "You should have seen the look on her face when I ripped it from her own skull."

I'm shaking, imaging the terror her daughter must have gone through in those brief moments. "You're sick…" I take a few steps backwards. "A parent is supposed to protect their children, what did your children ever do to you?"

Her face falls and anger spills across it. "They took *him* away from me. *He* was supposed to be mine. But no, he loved *them* all more than me! It was always *them*! What about *me*?" she screams, pushing an advancing biter to the ground and stomping on his skull. "They said it would be better once we had children, that it would bring us together…but the only thing it did was rip us apart!"

As much as I wanted Phoenix to get the satisfaction of killing Jerrica, she isn't here, and I can't just let her walk away. Not after everything. If I let her go, she'll just be back later. If I take her hostage, she'll just try to escape. *No, she deserves to suffer.* I shoot the gun in the air, startling her. She stops moving, eyeing the position of my rifle.

"You know, when we first found you, I took pity on you. We all did. We took you in as one of us, and we took care of you. And how did you betray us? By trying to get us killed…multiple times. And then we come to find out what you did to your own flesh and blood? Shooting you would be too kind." I take a few steps closer to her, my rifle still pointed at her head. "After everything you did, you don't deserve an ounce of leniency."

She breaks out into a wicked grin. "You've already admitted you're not going to shoot me. Why don't you admit that you don't have it in you," she taunts me. A few biters get too close for comfort and I quickly take them out before reaching into my back pocket for my knife. Jerrica is watching me intently. Although she claims I don't have it in me, she seems uneasy with my sudden movements. "You're the good guy, Ike, don't pretend to be anyone else."

I run the sleek metal between my fingers. "The thing is…I don't want to be the good guy anymore." And even though I only semi-believe the words coming out of my mouth, I lunge for her and she scrambles to get away. I take my blade to the back of her heels, slicing each one with absolute precision, she screams out in agony. I've immobilized her from running and she is in shock. She is grabbing at the back of her heels, where the blood is spilling out onto the yellowed and dead grass. "That was for Rian and Foster."

She is taking staggering breaths, cussing, and trying to crawl away, but she's no match for me. "This is for Phoenix and Cullen." I swiftly bring the blade across the side of her abdomen. Her screams only intensify as the blood begins to pool out her side. "And this…this is for your poor, unsuspecting children. I hope they are watching now." I take the knife and stab her directly in the throat, silencing her. She's still alive, but barely. I rip the knife roughly out of her throat as the red blood spills out and onto the grass beneath her.

I look up and there are biters closing in from every angle. In moments, she will be swarmed with them. I have no intention of leaving Neveah without a guardian, so I holster my knife and pick up my rifle. I empty a few more shots into the immediate threats and then begin walking away from her.

I make no effort of looking back. I can already hear the biters feasting on her flesh, ripping it from her body. By the time I reach the roadblock, I look around the ground and there is a mixture of dead Degenerates, and far too many teenagers from my group lying about. One of the remaining soldiers approaches me. "What was that?" He is motioning his head toward the field where I left Jerrica.

"Nothing important. Help me clear a path, will ya?" I feel terrible for how many we lost to the Degenerates today, but I consider it a victory that I not only eliminated Earl, but Jerrica too.

I know this will never make up for all the damage she has caused, but it's a start. Someone finally had the chance to stand up for her children who never had a chance. I'm thankful that someone was me.

Rest in peace, kids.

Eighteen – Beauty and the Beast

Cullen

I have managed to find myself in quite the predicament, surrounded by biters, but it could be worse. I'm lucky that they are all wearing helmets with faceguards and the most damage they can do to me currently is surround me. I've managed to kick quite a few of them to the ground, but, even without arms, they eventually find a way to get back on their feet again. They're much more resilient than I would have guessed.

I hear the guards dragging someone down the pathway, and notice it is President Jackson. He is hunched over, and it looks as if he's been badly beaten. I watch as they open the cage across from mine, the one Phoenix is locked up in, and they throw President Jackson to the ground.

"President Cruz is requesting your presence at dinner," I hear one of the guards say and I crane my neck around the biters pressing into me, trying to get a glimpse of whom they are speaking to.

"Tell him to go to hell," the familiar voice responds, and my stomach drops. *Phoenix*.

I hear what sounds like a physical altercation, and then gasps and whispers among the others in the cage with Phoenix.

"You can either come with us willingly like a good girl, or we can make you, it's your choice," the soldier replies. "I'm fine with either. I'd love to get my hands dirty with you."

I know the longer she protests, the worse it will be for her. I'm grasping at the metal bars that hold me in, silently hoping she will do as they say. Biters are pressing up on me, and I am shoving them out of the way. *Come on, Phoenix; don't get yourself killed.*

A few moments later I hear the cage being locked back up, and a stampede of footsteps. Four soldiers lead Phoenix toward the elevator. She stops walking and locks eyes with me for a brief second before they shove her forward.

"No! Phoenix!" I cry, pounding on the metal cage I'm locked up in. I have no idea what he wants with her. I never gave up any information about her being immune, and if they aren't aware of that, then it worries me even more. The idea that the stare I just shared with her, may be our last, fuels me with adrenaline. There are a handful of biters pressing up against me, their teeth hitting the plastic faceguard from their helmets. I grab two of them and slam them together roughly, sending them falling to the floor from impact. I kick my leg underneath another one and he falls on top of them. Wrapping my fingers around another biter's neck, I slam him against the metal bars and then throw him across the cage. More are still pushing to get close to me, but within moments, I have a pile of armless biters lying atop one another. They are temporarily immobilized.

I can feel eyes on me from across the walkway. I look up and multiple people housed in the opposite cage as me are wide-eyed and focused on the commotion I've made. I don't know whether to take a bow or say something. I decide to do neither as I slide down to the ground, breathing heavily.

* * *

Phoenix

I have no idea what I am in for when I am led from the basement and back to the main level. The soldiers shuffle me into one of the bedrooms, and I'm told to change into a blue ball gown which is lying on the expensive-looking bed. I can count on one hand the amount of times I've worn a dress in my life, not to mention one as extravagant as the one before me. It is midnight blue with silver beads and accents all along the bodice. There are no straps, and it has the biggest skirt I've ever seen. It looks like it came out of the Princess Diaries.

"Do you mind?" I ask with a bite to the two soldiers who are still in the room with me.

They grumble something back at me, but within seconds the door is closed, and I am left alone. Not wanting to waste another second, I race around the large room, looking for anything I can use to fight back with. Besides a closet full of luxurious clothes, I don't find anything. There is a window, which I run to, and begin trying to open, but it is almost as if it's glued shut. Either that or it's not a real window, more just for decoration. I slam my fist against it, letting out a throaty sob. *This was a mistake.* I sink to the floor, defeated. To think I just got Cullen back, only to lose him again because of my genius idea. I don't know how we are going to make it out of here alive.

My eyes travel along the walls and the ceilings, landing on a security camera in the far corner. Even if I wanted to escape, I'd guess they're watching me. They'd take me out before I even had a chance.

My one saving grace is that Ike isn't with us. He has a chance at survival. *I hope he doesn't have any more run-ins with Degenerates.* I know it's unlikely, but it's as positive as I can get in the current situation. I hear the door handle turning and I jump to my feet, unsure of who is walking in. The same soldiers who left me to change moments ago have returned, and by the looks on their faces they aren't happy with me. They pull out what looks to be aluminum police batons, and begin beating me with them. I fall to the ground in the fetal position, the hard objects coming in contact with my arms, legs, back, head, and stomach. After what feels like an eternity, they stop, but the pain remains.

I feel myself being lifted to my feet, and then my clothing is ripped from my body brutally. I am shaking when they bring the ball gown over my head and zip me up in it. I can already feel the bruises beginning to form all over my body.

I am led to a large dining room which has an elaborate large table, and a spread of food I could only dream of. There is an extravagant chandelier hanging from the ceiling, lighting up the entire spread. The smell of freshly cooked food fills my nostrils, and for a brief, fleeting moment, it reminds me of home. The spread before me could easily feed twenty-five people, if not more. I'm immediately angered, although my stomach rumbles loudly. I know they are feeding the prisoners little to nothing. Most of the people who were in the cage with me appeared to be starving to death. I'm sickened by the thought of it.

The soldiers pull out a chair for me to sit on, and they end up tying me up. The way the restraints are placed, I still have use of the lower part of my arms. The soldiers step away once they have secured me in place and a middle-aged man who is dressed in a pristine grey suit enters the room. He is wearing a white collared shirt and a blue tie to match my fancy ball gown. He has dark brown skin, and appears to be South American.

"You must be Phoenix," he addresses me as he crosses the room to my chair. He takes my hand, and presses his lips to it gently.

"Who are you?" I ask shortly.

"Well, isn't it obvious, my dear?" he asks, taking a seat at the other end of the large table. "I'm the President of the United States."

I blink a few times, digesting his words. I know without a shadow of a doubt that the real President is in the basement locked up. I'm not sure who this imposter is, but in a way I don't want to find out.

"You are more stunning than I could have ever imagined," he says, motioning toward his empty champagne glass. One of the soldiers steps forward with a bottle, and begins pouring it into his glass. "Champagne?"

I shake my head as if to say no, but don't bother using words.

"I trust that my men treated you well." He lifts the champagne glass to his lips, taking a drink.

"If you call a brutal beating well, then yes, they went above and beyond," I reply dryly, locking eyes with him.

His eyes widen as he slams his glass down on the table. "Nagel!" he shouts.

The secretary of defense comes running in, still dressed to the nines. "Yes, sir?"

"What is this that I hear about my guest being mistreated?" He speaks with authority and conviction, and I'm not surprised that he is running this entire operation.

Nagel glances at me nervously, and then back to him. "Sir, she wasn't cooperating. She was told to get dressed, and given more than enough time, but when they went to check on her, she was still in her dirty clothes."

The man in charge shifts his eyes to me and then back to Nagel. "Mmm-hmm." He scoots his chair back, and then makes his way back toward me. I feel his fingers grace my skin as he lifts up the large skirt of my dress, and he inspects my legs. He then grabs my arm, turning it over.

"Did I give the order to rough her up?" He stands up, taking a few steps toward his right hand man.

"No, sir, but…" Nagel doesn't get a chance to finish. He is shot in the head before I can even process a clear thought. The man then spins around, and puts a bullet in the three remaining soldiers' heads. My mind is racing. I have no idea what to expect now.

"Where were we?" he asks, setting his pistol on top of the table. "Oh, yes, I don't think we've been properly introduced. "I'm Jose Cruz."

I swallow, nodding. I know how quickly he turned on his own men, so I'm being extra careful about what comes out of my mouth.

"I don't know about you, but I'm famished," he says, motioning toward the elaborate spread before us. He returns back to his chair, and begins filling up his own plate.

My stomach rumbling loudly agrees with him, but, I can't with a good conscience eat, knowing that the others are suffering below us.

"What's the matter?" he asks, taking a big bite out of a bread roll. "Aren't you hungry?"

"Yes," I say, thinking about every word before it leaves my mouth, "but, I can't eat this food...not when I know there are people downstairs who need it more than I do."

He stops chewing, dropping the roll onto his plate. "Well, why didn't you say anything? Garcia!"

Another soldier races into the room, but nearly trips on the dead bodies lying about the floor. He stumbles backward, surprised by the sight. "President Cruz?"

"I need you to take some food to the prisoners."

"Sir?" he asks, seemingly hesitant. It's obvious his request is not common.

"You heard me. Grab a plate, and get some men to clean this up." He motions with his head toward the three deceased soldiers.

"Yes, sir." Garcia begins hastily filling up a

plate with an assortment of food before leaving the room.

"I would suggest you eat now, Phoenix. We don't know when you will get another chance like this one." I heed his advice. It doesn't take much to convince me, my salivating tongue already had its mind made up when I entered the large room.

Because I am still tied to the chair, I can only reach a number of the items on the table, but it's enough for me. I'm able to fill up my plate with an assortment of fruits, nuts, and veggies. Before the virus, I was a vegetarian. This is the closest I have been to it since. I savor it all. Once I have filled my stomach to my heart's content, I lean back, exhaling deeply. Jose's eyes are on me the entire time, as if he's drinking me up.

"Why did you bring me here?" I ask, attempting to tread lightly.

He shifts in his chair. "You were one of the ones who brought the cure, were you not? I thought this might be a good way to give back to you."

I snort. "If you wanted to repay us, you would let us go."

His jaw becomes tense. "Unfortunately, you both know too much at this point."

"Who would we tell?" I counter. "Have you looked outside? There's not much of a government left, if you haven't noticed."

He chuckles, throwing his cloth napkin onto the table. "I like you, Phoenix. You tell it like it is. You're much different than I imagined."

He makes it seem as if he's been thinking about me for a while.

"What would you say if I told you that you could have this lifestyle…with me?"

I nearly choke on my own surprise. *I would say that you're delusional.* Instead, I go with something that may or may not get me killed. "I know this may come as a shock to you, but, Cullen is my family now, and I would never leave him."

He breathes in deeply, seemingly agitated. "I thought you might say something like that." He scoots his chair out as a few soldiers enter the room, and begin cleaning up the blood and lifeless bodies of their mates. He grabs one of them by the arm, and whispers something into their ear.

The soldier begins walking toward me, and my stomach starts doing sickening flops. "It was very nice to meet you, Phoenix. I wish we could have met under better circumstances, but this is the reality of our life now." He buttons the bottom of his suit jacket and exits the room.

"Where are you taking me?" I ask frantically, as the soldier begins undoing my ties.

He doesn't bother answering me, as he grabs my arm aggressively and pulls me up. I'm taken back to the same bedroom I was assaulted in earlier. No soldiers remain in the room with me, as the door shuts with a click. I run to it, pulling, only to realize that they have locked me in. I have no idea what he has ordered them to do with me, and that is unsettling. I can't sit still. I begin pacing the room, back and forth, anxiously.

My eyes land back on the security camera and immediately, I begin thinking of ways to disarm it. They're smart enough not to leave any potential weapons lying about, so I rush into the bathroom and grab a plastic pitcher from underneath the sink, filling it up with steaming hot water. I find a chair and position it under the base of the camera and then I toss the steaming hot water directly at the piece of equipment. It begins cackling and sparking, and I know I've put it out of commission. I hop down from the chair, satisfied.

Not long after, the door opens, and a young teenager is thrown onto the ground in the room. The door closes and locks immediately after. He has shaggy black hair and acne, and appears no older than fifteen. I crouch down next to him, touching his arm lightly. "Hey, are you alright?"

He turns to face me, and there is panic in his stare. My eyes travel to the side of his neck where it is obvious he has been bitten. Now I understand the reason for his fear. I stumble backwards, unable to hide the look on my face, one of complete hopelessness.

"I'm going to die, aren't I?" he asks shakily, standing up. He presses the palm of his hand to his neck to attempt to stop the bleeding.

I swallow. I want to lie to him. I want to tell him everything is going to be okay, but I can't. He is going to die, and there isn't a damn thing I can do about it. My facial expression gives me up, and he begins hyperventilating.

"How long ago did that happen?" I ask, trying to sound casual.

"A few hours," he responds. His nose begins bleeding, and he looks up at me once again, the fear more than apparent. He wipes the blood away with the back of his hand before he glances back up. The veins in his eyes are beginning to pop, one by one.

They put him in here to kill me. Even though he's a young boy, I have no other choice than to defend myself. My eyes scan the room once more for anything I can use for a weapon. My heart is beating frantically, and I know I am running out of time.

"How could they do this to me?" he asks angrily. Agitation is beginning to take over, and I know it can't be much longer.

Moments later he is charging me, his fingers wrapping around my neck. "You did this!" he screams, strangling me. I am grasping at his fingers, trying to pry them off, but my air is wearing thin. I am gasping for breaths, when I finally manage to kick one of his legs out from under him and he falls. I reach my fingers up to my neck, breathing deeply.

He is making loud sobbing noises, and I know he is undergoing a range of emotions. Pretty soon, he has blood dripping from not only his nose, but now his eyes and mouth too. He is choking on his own blood. I'm angry that I don't have the antiserum to inject him with. I'm angry he is going to die at the hands of this sadistic bastard.

I kneel down next to him, cradling his head into my chest. "Shhh." I attempt to soothe him. I feel his teeth close down on my shoulder, and I cry out in pain, pushing him from me. He lands on the ground, barely moving, and his breathing becomes shallow. I know now that I only have minutes before he is fully transitioned into the walking dead. I jump to my feet and run to the long, narrow wooden bed posts. Hopping on the bed, I begin to kick at the posts with force until a piece the size of a cane breaks off. It's sharp and jagged, and I know it is going to be the one thing that will stand between me and the new biter. I don't wait for him to transition fully before I plow it through his skull. I release my grip on the weapon, and fall to my knees. "Please forgive me," I whisper sadly.

A few minutes later, the door opens and Jose enters. His eyes assess the room and he seems surprised, while also disappointed. "It's too bad that you got bit, Mama. We could have made a powerful couple."

"You're disgusting," I mutter under my breath. "You wouldn't have the antiserum if it weren't for us." I want him to believe that I am a lost cause. If anyone knows that I'm immune as well, I'd become another lab experiment.

"Because I'm such a nice guy, I'm going to give you the chance to say goodbye." Two soldiers come in the room, and grab me by each arm. I'm led through the long hallways, back down the stairwell and to the basement where I originally came from. But this time, instead of locking me up in the cage adjacent from Cullen, they throw me in the same one with him. They probably think they are killing two birds with one stone.

Cullen rushes to my side the minute I am inside with him. "Are you okay?" he asks worriedly, his hand immediately cupping my cheek, but his eyes scanning my shoulder.

I nod stiffly. "I'm fine." His eyes continue to rake over my injury. "Don't worry. No one knows."

"What are we going to do?" he asks.

I shrug. "I guess we're just going to have to hope for a miracle."

Nineteen – Something isn't Right

Ike

"What is that?" I ask as I slowly press down on the brakes. Jean-Luc cranes his neck to see what I am referring to.

"It looks like people…real people."

"I know," I reply shortly. "But, what are they all doing out on the street?"

We have encountered quite a few biters on our drive to Washington, but it didn't go unnoticed to me how much calmer things have been since we made it into the city. I have no idea if the people we see on the street are more Degenerates or simply citizens like us.

"What is the plan?" Jean-Luc asks as I bring the van to a full stop.

"I don't see any weapons in plain sight. At least not any guns. I am going to speak with them." I grab the rifle beside me, and reach for the door handle.

"Would you like me to back you up?" Jean-Luc

offers, already grabbing for his own door handle.

"No, I'd like you to stay here and make sure everyone is safe. I'm going to assess the situation." I hop out of the vehicle, closing the door behind me, catching the attention of a handful of eyes.

I approach a pair of men, both who are middle-aged like me. The first is dark-skinned, tall, and lanky. He looks African. The second is a blond haired, green eyed bulky male. He has a mustache attached to a massive beard. They are exchanging wary glances as I approach. I assume because of the fire power I carry with me.

"Hello," I say gently. "My name is Ike."

Again they exchange concerned glances before the bulky male speaks. "We don't have much, but take whatever you want. Just please, don't harm anyone here."

I look around, and there are more than twenty pairs of eyes trained on me. They are spread out around the street, and they appear to be keeping watch. Although their attention has now shifted completely to me.

The way they react tells me they aren't

Degenerates, but I've been wrong in the past. "I'm not here to take anything from you," I say, dropping my rifle to my side. "We are headed to the White House."

The dark-skinned male exhales loudly. "You've heard about the cure. Are you planning on trading for it?"

My eyebrows furrow with concern. "What do you know about the cure?"

He puts his hands up in surrender. "Just the word on the street." His accent is thick, and I wonder how long he's been in the United States.

I don't have time to worry about his heritage, because what they are saying makes me uneasy. "Tell me what you know."

The blond male takes a step forward, but it is not aggressive. "Look, man, we know what everyone else around here knows. Soldiers came out a couple of days ago, spreading a message about the President manufacturing a working cure. They mentioned there is only a limited supply, and they are for sale to the highest bidders."

The uneasy feeling continues to grow inside of me. "What good would money do to them now? The President should have enough of that left over anyway."

"Not money," he replies. His eyes graze over my rifle and things are beginning to make sense.

If the President is trading the cure for weapons and ammo, then I fear the worst for Cullen and Phoenix. They wouldn't have given it up without a fight.

I look around, noticing their group has been quietly taking out biters the entire time we've been conversing.

"What do you know of a red haired female and a blond, muscular male?" I ask.

The pair look at each other and back to me. "They came through here last week. The soldiers let them into the White House. We haven't seen them since."

My stomach begins churning.

"Thank you for this information." I begin to walk back to the van when the deep voice of the taller one stops me.

"There's something you should know."

I turn back around slowly.

"There is someone calling the shots in there." He points with his head in the general direction of the White House. "But it's not the President."

I narrow my eyes. "Who is it then?"

He shrugs his shoulders. "No one knows. He never steps foot outside of the gates. But the soldiers refer to him as President Cruz."

I swallow. Phoenix and Cullen had no idea what they were walking into. For all I know, Degenerates have taken up residence in the White House, and we just blindly gave them the cure. I can only hope and pray that they are still alive.

"Thank you," I say once more as I walk with a faster pace toward the van.

As soon as I hop in, all attention is on me. You can hear a pin drop, it's so silent.

"What happened?" Jean-Luc asks on behalf of the entire group.

"I don't think they are Degenerates. I'm not sure if we can trust them either, but they willingly gave me some information." I pause, debating the next words out of my mouth. "Phoenix and Cullen are in danger. Someone inside those confines is parading around as the President."

Gasps come from every corner of the van. "He has the cure and he is offering trades for weapons and ammo."

Jean-Luc's eyes go wide. "How do we even know they are still alive?"

I shrug, turning the key to start the engine. "I guess we are just going to have to have a little bit of faith."

*   *   *

We park around the corner from the White House, keeping a safe distance. After congregating and agreeing on a plan, we split the group in half, leaving only three weapon-yielding teenagers and Jean-Luc behind to care for the women and children. I take the rest of the group, all which are equipped with firearms like me, and we approach on foot. We have agreed to keep our identity a secret, and instead decide that if asked, we will lead them to believe we are a group that came from Knoxville. There will be no mention of Cullen, Phoenix, or Jean-Luc. I know we are not walking into safe conditions. I know the soldiers they spoke of will be similarly equipped with guns.

The group I lead knows to let me speak; let me do the negotiating. I have to get inside somehow. Whether they allow my group along with me, will be up to them. I notice one group of soldiers guarding the side gate, while another group takes out biters that are lined up along the metal fence.

"Keep your weapons at your side," I order as we approach hesitantly. The guards take notice of us almost immediately. They approach the fence just as we arrive.

"I'm here to speak about a trade," I say, gripping my rifle tightly to my side.

The soldiers are dressed in full military gear along with helmets and plastic faceguards. I'm unsure of why they are dressed as if they are in war, but it occurs to me that they are simply taking every precaution possible.

"How many weapons do you have there?" One of the soldiers asks me, beckoning with his head toward my group.

"Does it matter?" I ask. "I have weapons and ammo, and I heard that you have the cure."

They swivel their heads between each other and then back to us. "Pass the weapons through."

I snort. "You're asking me to give up the only leverage we have for...what? Your word? I think we'll hold onto our weapons until you get me the cure."

The soldier who has been corresponding with me sighs loudly. "The President will want to meet you to finalize the deal."

I look up at the thick metal gate separating us. "Then I guess you're going to have to open up."

They open the gate within seconds. We begin to advance when the soldiers raise their guns, pointing them straight at us. "You'll have to forgive us for being wary, but, the President likes his privacy." The solider nods his head at me. "You. The President will meet with you, and you alone."

I nod my head in understanding. I can tell my people are nervous, but I turn around, addressing them. "It's alright. I'm going to be fine. Stay here. If I'm not out within thirty minutes, take whatever precautions necessary to get out of here, unharmed."

"Jonathan," I grab his head and pull his ear to my lips. "If I don't return, you're in charge."

He nods his head, a solemn look taking over his face. He is the only remaining soldier we have left. I know he will do everything in his power to keep our people safe. I hand him my rifle, knowing they aren't going to let me take it in.

I know there is a great possibility I am walking into a trap, but I am doing it for Cullen. If the roles were reversed and I was the one missing, he'd travel through hell and high water to find me; dead or alive.

Four soldiers break away, leading me into the enormous mansion, and the rest staying guard at the fence. I steal one more glance at my group before I am secured inside the colossal walls. The soldiers pat me down, finding a knife in my boot and tossing it before they begin leading me through a series of hallways. They stop in front of a big, ivory door, and then open it. I recognize the room immediately, it is the Oval Office.

"Go on," one of the soldiers motions with his hand. I scoot past him and into the large room as the door closes behind me. I hear gurgling noises and swivel around to find two biters, one at each end of the room, secured by chains.

They have no arms and they are wearing identical helmets to the soldiers outside the door. By the looks of it, they appear to be some kind of rabid pet for the person in charge.

I'm not sure who is calling the shots around here, but I can take a guess that they have some screws loose. I step away from the biters, further into the room, but it is quiet. No one else is present in the room. My eyes dart around, quickly. A few years ago, it would have felt like such an honor being in the infamous office. It saddens me to think how much has changed in the last few months. I wonder if the President is still alive. I wonder if he made it out before the infection spread.

I hear a side door open, and a tan-skinned gentleman steps through. He has short black hair and is dressed in what I can only deduce as one hell of an expensive suit. I know immediately this is the man in charge.

He nods his head in my direction. "You must be here to trade for the cure."

I nod my head in agreement.

"Well, what are you offering?" He strides toward me, taking a seat on one of the couches in the middle of the room.

"We have rifles, pistols, ammo."

He bobs his head up and down. "All things I'm very much interested in. What's your name?"

"Ike," I reply.

I don't want the cure in the least, what I'd like to know is where my friends are; what he's done with them.

"Well, Ike, how many doses of the cure are you looking for?"

I act like I'm pondering his question, as my eyes trail the room. I'm looking for any signs of a struggle. Any signs that will tell me if Phoenix and Cullen have been in this room before. Any signs to let me know that they are still alive.

"Just one," I lie. I need to buy time. I need information from him.

He nods, his eyebrows furrowing. "That shouldn't be a problem. Do you mind waiting here?"

I shake my head as he stands up and begins retreating back to the door he originally walked through.

I know my time is up. I slink behind him, and before he knows it, I have him in a headlock. He doesn't even know what has hit him. He's fighting against me, wrestling for his freedom, but my hold is strong. I can feel his fingers grasping at my arms, trying to pull them away from his neck. "Who are you?" he hisses.

I don't budge an inch. He's strong, but I'm stronger. "The better question to ask is, who the hell are you?"

"Guards!" he screams, alerting his soldiers from outside the door. I know I'm more than likely dead, but I have leverage.

The door flies open and I'm met with an array of guns all pointed straight at me. I do my best to keep my body behind their leader. My head is still exposed, but with the hold I have around his head, I assume they will think twice before making any rash moves.

"Let him go!" one of the soldiers orders in a firm tone.

I move my hand to the side of his head. "Take one more step, and I snap his neck."

I can feel his heartbeat pressed up against my chest, and I know I have the upper hand.

"Don't shoot!" he barks, his tone authoritative.

"There was a redheaded female and a blond male who came here a few days ago. The word on the street is you let them in, but they never came back out. Where are they?"

The man in my arms begins to chuckle, almost sadistically. "I should have known you were one of *them*."

My stomach drops as I tighten my hold. He begins gasping, choking for air. The soldiers with their guns pointed at me become more agitated and tense. "I'm sorry, I didn't quite catch that."

I loosen my hold enough that he is able to speak. "They are alive."

I nod, stiffly. "Take me to them."

I feel a gun being pressed up to the back of my skull. "You're going to want to release him now."

My heart begins pounding inside my chest as I realize I've lost my upper-hand. I release my hold on him, and he gasps for breath, rubbing his hand across his neck gingerly.

"I'm sorry, I don't think we were properly

introduced," the tanned man says, straightening his suit jacket. I watch as he grabs one of the rifles from the bunch. "I'm President Cruz." And then I see the butt of the rifle come barreling at my face, blackness following.

Twenty – A New Plan

Ike

I come to on a cold, hard surface. The first thing I see are Phoenix's bright blue eyes staring down at me. "Phoenix?" I ask, as my eyes adjust.

She cradles my head in her lap and I see relief wash over her face. "You stupid, old man."

My head is aching from the impact of the gun, and I shakily reach my hand up, feeling the welt that is forming on my forehead. I see someone moving from the corner of my eye and I turn my head. "Cullen."

"Hey, boss," he greets me with a solemn look on his face. He reaches his hand out and I take it as he lifts me to my feet.

"How are you feeling, Phoenix? Have the chills started yet? How about the insatiable hunger?" I hear the familiar voice from the leader of the soldiers'.

Phoenix looks up. "Go to hell."

"You're lucky I believe in the power of

goodbyes."

Before I can focus fully on his words, I notice we are not alone. There are a horde of biters, decayed skin and all, in the small confined area along with us. They are all wearing helmets similar to the ones in the Oval Office, and not one of them has any arms. They are pressing up against me, and I can hear the chattering of their teeth, as they press against the plastic faceguards. I push a few roughly away as I look the fake President directly in the eye.

"I guess I should be thanking you, then?" I say, sarcastically.

He breaks out into an evil grin. "Not yet, but you will. You know, I happened to spot a van full of women and children outside. Are they yours?"

My heart begins beating fast as I remember my group posted outside the gates. They won't stand a chance against these soldiers. "Don't you touch them!" I scream, pressing myself up against the metal bars we are locked up in, and reaching my arms out for him.

He grabs my arm, the same one that is only semi-healed and twists it until it snaps. I cry out in pain, falling to my knees, breathing heavily.

"Here's what's going to happen," Cruz responds in a calculated tone. "We're going to take your women and your guns. We're going to rape them in front of you, and then we are going to kill you." I hear gasps originate from another part of the room and realize we are not alone. My wild eyes travel over Cruz's head, and I see another cage filled with a multitude of people. Their facial expressions read fear and panic.

I lock eyes with Cruz once more before he walks away, grabbing his arm with my one good hand. "I'm going to kill you."

He smiles darkly before prying my fingers from his arm. "Go get them."

The soldiers scurry out the door and he follows, rounding up the back. He turns back once to look at me, reveling in his win before he shuts the door loudly.

I feel hands underneath my armpit, lifting me to my feet. My knees feel weak. I led my people here, and now they are going to suffer because of me. The pain from my arm is no comparison to the pain I feel in my heart. I can hear someone saying my name, but it sounds garbled and far away. I can't focus on anything but the notion that I've just led my people to their death.

I feel hands on my shoulders, shaking me roughly. "Ike! Ike!"

I look up, defeated.

Cullen is staring down into my face, a concerned look spread across his own. "Ike, snap out of it!" he orders, slapping me roughly. "You can't give up. Those people are counting on you."

I swallow, dread filling my insides. "There's nothing we can do now."

Cullen's gaze narrows, anger apparent in his stare. "*You* taught me to never give up. Where there's a will, there's a way, remember?"

Sounds like something the old Ike would say. I don't even recognize myself anymore.

"We need a plan," I hear Phoenix say.

Cullen removes his hands from my shoulders, and then steps closer to the metal bars. He is looking out across the way toward the other group of people locked up. I'm watching him, but unsure of what he is thinking. His eyes shift all over the place as he becomes lost in thought. "I think I have an idea. You!" He motions to a woman in the other metal cage. "How many of those hairpins do you have?"

She reaches up to her delicately styled light brown hair, and then stares back at him. "Three, maybe four, why?"

"Throw me two."

Her expression still reads confusion as she carefully pulls them from her hair, and then tosses them across and into our cage. Cullen immediately grabs them from the ground, and begins prying them open.

"What are you going to do?" Phoenix asks curiously.

"I'm going to get us out of here, and we're going to save our people." Once he has both hairpins straightened out, we watch as he takes them to the lock on the other side of the metal door. He is twisting and turning them, and after multiple attempts, I'm ready to call it quits and simply wallow in our combined loss. Cullen doesn't give up as easily, making me wonder where he gets it from. I'm no inspiration or role model.

When the click finally sounds, I think my heart bursts. With wide eyes, the three of us all exchange wary glances. It's as if none of us can believe he's actually pulled it off. He pushes on the door lightly, and it swings open. Loud gasps come from the adjacent cage, and whispers are beginning to turn into full-blown begs.

"Shhh," Cullen orders, silencing them with his finger against his lips. "We'll get you out of here, I promise. He slips out of our cage quietly, and begins wrestling with the lock on the other cage. Because he can actually see what he is doing this time, it's only moments before the lock is undone.

"What now?" Phoenix asks, her eyes locked on the door the soldiers walked out of.

My eyes immediately travel to the corners of the room, searching for any of the security cameras I saw along the hallways and in the Oval Office. I locate two separate ones, and quickly find the end of a mop to use to disable them. "We don't have much time," I warn the rest of the group.

"Mr. President?" A familiar looking figure steps out of the cage, and my eyes widen as I realize the President of our nation is still alive. He looks worn out and weak, but he is breathing.

The room becomes eerily quiet as he addresses the lot of us. "They locked me up without bothering to find out more information about the place they've been calling their home for the past few months. There are secret passageways they haven't found yet. We are going to need to be quick, and we are going to need to be quiet."

I take a few steps toward the other cage, my heart beating out of my chest. "Get your people out, we will be right behind you."

All eyes swivel around to focus on me. "Cullen, Phoenix, help me create a distraction."

Phoenix breathes out a sigh of relief, her hand reaching out to my shoulder. "It's good to have you back."

The President begins shuffling his people out of the cage, and they make their way to a back wall. I watch as he pulls down on a fire extinguisher, and a hidden door slides open. A large room filled with an assortment of deadly weapons is exposed. He begins pushing people through the entryway as Cullen and Phoenix meet back up with me.

"What's your plan?" Cullen asks, keeping his eyes peeled.

I motion with my head toward the biters. "Let's put them to good use."

We lead the armless biters to the elevator,

holding them in with a stick across the door and then press the button for the main level. Loud bangs and booms carry down from above; rapid gunfire. We remove the helmets from each biter, one at a time, and continue holding them off until we can get the door secured and closed. It isn't an easy feat, but we manage to do it without being bitten. When we have finished securing them inside the elevator, we locate a rope to secure the door to the stairwell. It won't hold them off for long, but it will give us a head start.

By the time we reach the secret room, every single person is equipped with a weapon of their own. We slip inside as the President pulls on the fire extinguisher once more and the door slides shut. My eyes widen at the sight of the room. It has to be the deadliest room in the entire mansion. If Cruz even knew it existed, he'd have no need to bargain with the people on the streets. There are pistols, rifles, automatic weapons, Uzi's, and grenade launchers among many others.

"What is your weapon of choice?" President Jackson asks Phoenix. She smiles. "Give me one of the machine guns."

I shake my head as I scan the options myself, trying to decide before I am asked. Cullen opts for an Uzi and the President hands me the grenade launcher.

"How did you know?" I ask, my hand sliding over the sleek, heavy metal.

"The look of revenge in your eyes," he answers simply.

I nod.

With the current situation of my arm, there is no way in hell I will be able to lift the damn thing, but I admire it for a few brief moments before opting for something more practical like a machine gun.

He grabs two large bags and instructs the men of his Secret Service team to fill them up with as many weapons and ammo as they can fit. They do so quickly, and then he pulls on a lamp located on the wall which opens another hidden door. This time, a hallway greets us. "I never used these secret passageways when I was in office, but I guess there's a first time for everything," he states as he ushers everyone through the hallways.

He is leading a deadly army; a force to be reckoned with. Apart from his Secret Service, which looks to be around thirty men, there are another fifty of us in the group. No one will stand a chance against us and the manpower we have now.

Looking at everyone heavily armed gives me a sense of relief. I feel as though we will all have our revenge.

Twenty One – The Take Over

Cullen

The President leads us out of the secret passageway, directly into the Oval Office. I'm not too keen on the idea at first because it puts us directly in the middle of all the gun commotion, but we are surprised to find the office completely empty minus the biters still chained up. The loud gunfire is still sounding off in the hallway, and I can only assume that the group Ike left behind outside has decided to open fire.

I shoot at the cameras inside the room, disabling them. I know the noise may very well give us away, but we can take no chances.

We have more than enough ammo and guns to feel safe, but without knowing exactly what we are walking into, we are hesitant. The Secret Service insists that they need to secure "the package" and they rush him out a side entrance off the Oval Office. There are still fifty of us left and well-armed to leave a dent. I peek out the door of the office, and there are dead bodies scattered everywhere. Bullet holes adorn the door, walls, floor, and even ceiling. I can see shots being fired down the hall, but they are no longer in a close vicinity to the office.

We slink out, one by one, holding our weapons high, and make our way down the long hallway, stepping over the lifeless bodies. Ike's eyes are wide, taking in the sight. There are not only dead soldiers, but also dead teenagers that I recognize from back at the prison. There are a few injured soldiers who are pleading for us to help them, to which we respond by putting them out of their misery.

As we round the corner to the main entrance and large lobby area, the shots die off. I notice a fairly large group of people all tied up in the corner, with Jean-Luc and Neveah smack dab in the middle of it. We rush to them quickly, freeing them from their ties. It's all the women and children Cruz had threatened. "Are you alright?" Ike asks Neveah as he frees her from her ties.

She nods her head timidly, wrapping her arms around his neck.

Where are the rest?" Ike asks Jean-Luc, to which he responds by shaking his head solemnly.

Ike lets out a sob before throwing his hand over his mouth to stifle his surprise. He pulls

Neveah's arms away from his neck and his eyes immediately begin raking the floor for our fallen comrades. "Where is he?" he asks in a harsh tone, obviously looking for the whereabouts of Cruz.

Jean-Luc points to a door of the side wall, which is closed.

Ike marches toward it, his assault rifle pointed directly at it.

"Whoa, whoa, whoa!" I chase after him, slapping my hand on his shoulder. "Don't do this." I motion with my head back toward a frightened Neveah who now has her head and eyes buried into Jean-Luc's side. "You have priorities now. You have people counting on you." He looks back at me, his eyes full of sadness, and then his eyes sweep over to Neveah, guilt washing over his face. He drops the weapon to his side. It appears I've gotten through to him.

Phoenix comes up beside us. "Look, I know you want to kill him, but I want this kill for myself. Can you let me take this one?"

Ike looks at her with glazed over eyes before nodding his head slowly. If it were me, I wouldn't have given up the kill for anything, but I know he has a soft spot for Phoenix.

We both watch her carefully as she opens fire on the door and around it, a spray of bullets leaving their mark.

"I surrender!" we hear someone scream from inside the minute she stops.

I close in on the door and kick it open, finding a crouched Cruz inside. He is bleeding from the shoulder, and is panting. I rip him up from the ground, and pull him closer to Phoenix.

"Please!" he begs. "I'll do anything you want."

Phoenix stands before him, stone cold and stiff. She puts the end of his machine gun beneath his chin, lifting it up so he is staring back at her. "You messed with the wrong people."

He begins groveling almost immediately. "Please, Phoenix, I know you're not a killer."

Phoenix's jaw tenses and then she looks at Ike. "Get them out of here." She is motioning with her head toward the women and children. Ike nods in understanding as he begins ushering them down the hallway and out of eyesight.

Phoenix looks at me. "You sure you want to stay for this?"

I nod. I have no intention of moving an inch. "We're in this together, love."

Her lips curls up into a small smile, and then she turns her attention back on Cruz. "It seems that we are at a crossroads," she speaks slowly.

His eyes meet hers, and a look of confusion passes across them. "I want more than anything in the world right now to blow your brains away, but your blood is pure, like mine. Thus, my conundrum."

Cruz's forehead wrinkles as he digests her information. "Oh my God..." he trails off. "It can't be." He stumbles up quickly to his feet, still holding his shoulder.

"What? Too dense to catch on? Or maybe you were just too preoccupied with your hunger for power," Phoenix taunts him.

He doesn't bother answering, and his shifty eyes tell me he is going to make a run for it. Sure enough, moments later he takes off in a sprint toward the front door. Phoenix doesn't even hesitate, shooting him in the back of the leg. He falls to the floor, crying out in pain, and begins crawling toward the exit.

Phoenix walks up to him, slowly. "You can't leave, Cruz, this is your home. And you've just become our newest science experiment." She raises her automatic rifle in the air before slamming it down into his face, his body going limp.

She steals a glance at me and my eyebrows are raised.

"What?" she asks with a bite.

"Nothing." I shrug. "Has anyone ever told you how sexy you are when you take the reins?"

She blushes from my compliment. I'm not sure how I'm so turned on at this exact moment either, but I can guess it has something to do with the fiery redhead standing before me.

"Well? Are you just going to stand there and ogle me, or are you going to help me get him to the lab?" I chuckle as I shake my head, and begin moving toward her.

* * *

"The President is ready for you," one of the Secret Service agents informs us.

After we secured Cruz and made sure the rest of our gang was safe, we helped the President's security team haul out all of the dead bodies. We were told upon finishing that the President requested to meet with us.

Ike, Phoenix, and I enter the Oval Office, and I'm not surprised to see the previously chained up biters have been killed and disposed of. The only evidence that they were even here is some black, blood spatter and the chains they were bound by. As we enter the office, the President is seated at his desk, facing us. "Take a seat."

We do as we are told and each sit down next to one another on one of the couches in the middle of the room. President Jackson stands and then begins making his way around the desk toward us. As he approaches the front of it, he sits on the edge, leaning on it. "I don't know any other way to say it than you three saved my life, and the lives of my staff members, and because of this, I am indebted to you."

He lifts himself off of his desk and approaches us. "Please tell me what I can do to help repay you."

Phoenix, Ike, and I exchange glances before Ike takes the opportunity to speak. "Mr. President..."

"Please call me, Douglas," the President interrupts him.

"Um, Douglas, sir, the most important thing for my people right now is shelter and food."

"Done," President Jackson replies without hesitation. "Anything else?"

We exchange another glance, unsure of what else we should be requesting. "Maybe a change of clothes," Phoenix jokes, looking down at her dirty, elaborate gown.

The President chuckles. "Whatever you want, it's yours."

I sigh softly. "We appreciate that, we do, but what we really came here for, was a chance at rebuilding our nation."

The President's eyes grow wide. "And how would you propose we begin doing that?"

"Well, we came here with a cure, and we intend to continue manufacturing it as long as the blood supply lasts. Which unfortunately means, we have to keep Cruz alive."

President Jackson breathes in deeply. "Although I'd like nothing more than to see him dead, I understand the bigger picture." He moves over to the couch across from us. "How about a nice dinner to begin discussing our shared future?"

Phoenix lets out a giggle. "Thank God, because I'm starving!"

We all laugh, and I realize it's the first time any of us have felt safe enough to let go of our inhibitions.

"Truman!" the President barks, and one of his Secret Service agents scurries in the door. "Tell Lupita we are going to need to prepare enough food for everyone."

"Yes, sir," the agent nods before rushing back out the door.

"Now, where were we?"

Twenty Two – This Can't Be the End

Ike

"Look what I found!" I wave my hand in the air, holding out a Creamsicle.

Neveah's eyes grow wide with excitement as she runs over to me and snatches it out of my hand.

"What do you say?" I prompt her in a stern voice.

"Thank you, Mr. Glass." She begins opening the Popsicle, the plastic crinkling loudly.

"You know, I've been thinking, how would you like to call me Ike?" I ask, sitting down on the edge of the bed in the suite the President set me up with.

She looks up from the orange dessert nodding enthusiastically.

"Good." I chuckle. "I'd like that as well."

"Ike," she says, trying it on for size. She takes a deep breath and then looks down sadly. I stand up and saunter over to her, crouching down.

"You miss your mother, don't you?"

She nods, a silent tear trailing down her face. I gently tuck some strands of her hair behind her ear. "Me too. Do you know what I like to do when I get sad about her?"

She looks up, her emerald eyes locking onto mine. "What?"

"I think about all of the things I liked about her and it makes me smile. Want to try?"

She nods, wiping her tears away.

"Well, I always liked her smile, it was so inviting." I pause, remembering it. "Your turn."

"She was funny," Neveah says sadly.

"You're right, she was always making me laugh. Good one. My turn?" I point to myself for clarification.

She bobs her head in agreement. "Okay, I really liked her hugs."

Neveah smiles. "She gave the best hugs." I

wrap my arm around Neveah, tucking her head under my chin. I know I'm never going to be able to replace her mother or her father even, but I am going to do the best job I can with being her guardian.

* * *

Phoenix

As the hot water cascades off my back and the steam rises, the condensation covering the clear shower doors, I savor each and every moment under the faucet. The water is nearly scalding, but it barely phases me as I continue to wash off the built up dirt and grime I've accumulated over the past couple of days.

I remain in the shower until the water goes cold, after my skin becomes wrinkly, and I've been sitting on the ground for what feels like an eternity. After, I locate a toothbrush and toothpaste and spend the next twenty minutes brushing until my gums aren't bleeding any longer and I can taste the freshness from my teeth and tongue.

All of this feels like a dream, but I am taking full advantage of it. If it is all a dream that I am going to wake up from, at least I will be fully satisfied. I end up pulling my wet hair back into a loose braid, in an attempt to move it out of my face. After drying off, I locate clothes in the closet that are close enough to my size, I nearly rejoice. It's been so long since I've been in normal clothes, I can't help the stupid grin that forms across my lips and remains there until we are called down to the dinner.

Before that happens, I manage to slip out and downstairs to the laboratory, where they are keeping Jose. When I enter, Jean-Luc is there along with another five scientists all in white lab coats. "How are things going?" I ask as I step further into the white room.

Jean-Luc glances at me, a small smile forming upon his lips. "Phoenix…you look great."

I blush, pulling at the edge of the white t-shirt I'm in. "You're just saying that because you have to."

He laughs. "You look good cleaned up."

"Thanks." I shrug off his compliment. My eyes wander past him to Jose who is strapped down to one of the examination tables. I begin taking small steps toward him. He is awake and doesn't look to be weak. "What's going on?" I ask, in a timid voice.

Jean-Luc steps forward, placing himself to my right. "We've taken all the blood we can for today. Right now, we are simply waiting for his blood cells to replenish."

Jose turns his face to look at me, his eyes widening. "You have no idea who she is, do you?" he cries at Jean-Luc.

We exchange wary glances, and I peek back at the other scientists in the room, all of whom seem to be minding their own business.

"Shut up," I say under my breath.

"She's immune too! What are you doing? You could be manufacturing twice the amount of antiserum between the two of us!" Without hesitation, I knock him out with my elbow, ending his tirade against me.
My eyes wander back to the scientists, only this time, I know they heard him, as they are all staring in my general direction.

"What are you doing?" Jean-Luc scolds them. "Get back to work!"

They scurry back to their duties, but my heart is in overdrive. I have no idea what they will do with the information they just received. As much as I'd like to believe the President owes me, I can't be naïve enough to think that this is something he will be willing to look over.

"Go back upstairs," Jean-Luc orders me under his breath. "Make sure you're not alone."

I nod, glancing up at the security cameras on the walls. They are definitely on judging by the green blinking light, but I have no idea if the audio works or not. I guess I will just have to remain hopeful.

As I enter the elevator and the doors close, calming music begins to play. It's enough to slow my irregularly beating heart temporarily. We saved the President's life. We freed his staff. Even if he is to find out about my blood, I hope that he will approach the situation through rational eyes. It's disconcerting how quickly things can change. How safe I can feel one moment, and how vulnerable I can be the next. My only saving grace is that I have two men who will protect me with their lives, I just hope it won't come to that.

* * *

Cullen

After we have had a chance to change, eat, and clean up, we make our way back to the rooms the President has set up for us. Some of our group have to share rooms, but President Jackson goes all out for our three bedrooms.

They are all on the same level as his own bedroom, and they are beyond enormous.

Earlier, at dinner, we were able to begin discussing a plan to slowly rid each city in Washington of biters. We are going to attack the issue slowly at first, and then more aggressively. The first order of business is to invite all of the citizens from beyond the gate inside the premises to receive a vaccination. The second order of business is to begin securing communities where we can house all of the vaccinated citizens safely. Once we can clearly assess each skill level of the remaining citizens, we can go back to work on getting running electricity and water. It's not going to be easy, and it's definitely not going to be a quick transition, but we are going to return the world to how it should be.

I peer out the window of my large suite, down at the lawn of the White House where there are Secret Service agents posted around the edges of the building, armed and ready, and another handful of them out by the gates, taking down the biters. I exhale loudly, walking back to the large queen-sized bed and then plopping down on it. It feels like I am sleeping on clouds. I can't remember the last time I slept on such a comfortable mattress. I place my hands behind my head, closing my eyes just as I hear a soft knock on the door. "Come in," I say lazily, not wanting to move a muscle. I open my eyes slowly, unsure if I want to give up on my rest so easily.

Ike pops his head in, his eyes wandering around.

"Ike," I greet him as he lets himself in, closing the door behind him.

"Cullen," he replies stiffly.

"What's going on?" I ask, sitting up. The tone of his voice has me on edge.

He takes a few hesitant steps forward. "I ran into Jerrica and Earl on the way here."

"Fuck," I exhale the word loudly. "What happened?"

He looks distressed. "I couldn't let them walk away...not after everything."

I sigh, running a hand through my hair. "Phoenix is not going to be happy."

"I know," he replies. "I'm going to tell her. I'm just not sure this is exactly the right time."

I nod. "You're probably right. Give it one night, at least. She deserves to be happy for this one night."

He swallows, turning back toward the door. "Hey, Ike?" I call out for him before he has a chance to exit.

"Yeah?" He turns back around.

"Did you give them hell?"

He grins back at me slowly. "Complete."

I sigh, reveling in the fact that they died slow, painful deaths. After what we heard about Jerrica, it's the least of what she deserves.

A few minutes after Ike leaves my door is once again slightly opened, and Phoenix's red head pops in. "Hey," she says softly. She lets herself in, closing the door behind her.

"How's your room?" I ask.

She nods. "Comfortable. You?"

I shrug. "Same."

She takes a few steps toward my bed, and then takes a seat on the edge of it. She has changed out of the elaborate blue gown, and is now simply in a pair of jeans and a loose-fitting white V-neck t-shirt. I prefer her better this way.

"Is something bothering you, love?" I ask, as I sit up.

She shakes her head. "I want to believe it's this easy…but I'm hesitant." Even though she says otherwise, I can feel the uneasiness dripping off her. I know more than anyone that this all seems too good to be true, but for the first time in a long time, I want to believe it.

I take her hand in mine, rubbing it softly with my thumb. "You forget that none of this has been easy. We've been through hell, and we made it. It's time for something good."

She smiles slightly, looking down. I reach my hand out to cradle the side of her face. "At least one good thing came out of the darkness."

"And what was that?" she asks.

"You."

The minute the word leaves my mouth she locks eyes with me, holding me in an intense stare. "I don't know if I could have made it through all of this without you."

I scoot in closer, sweeping some of her hair from her face. "You don't give yourself enough credit. You're tough as nails, Phoenix, and it's dead sexy."

Her cheeks grow red as she looks down. "Why is it so hard for you to take a compliment?" I ask, tipping her chin back up so I can look her in the eyes.

She shrugs it off. "Good things don't happen to people like me."

"People like you?" I press. "From where I'm sitting you're one hell of a person. I've never met anyone like you. You're incredible."

Her lips are on mine before I can finish, kissing me hungrily. I pull her head in closer, deepening the kiss. She moans in my mouth and it drives me insane. "Hold that thought," I pull away and say, pressing my forehead to hers. I hop up and run to the door, turning the lock on the handle. I proceed to remove my own shirt and end up throwing it over the camera in the far corner of the room. "Sorry, guys, no show for you tonight."

When I turn back around, Phoenix has already shed her t-shirt and it is lying on the floor. My eyes flick between the floor and her exposed chest. It's not the first time I've seen it…or the second, but it feels like the most powerful time, because for the first time I can say that I am without a doubt, unequivocally head over heels in love with the woman standing before me. She is reaching for the button of her jeans when I race to her, putting my hand on hers, stopping her.

"What is it?" she asks, confused.

I look down at her, peering into her deep blue eyes. "I need you to know something before we go any further."

She swallows nervously, her eyes shifting away from mine as she takes a step back. "What?"

I soak her up once more with my eyes before I part my lips to speak. "I've never met anyone like you, Phoenix…" I begin, but she interrupts me.

"We've been over this before. A few times."

I inhale. "Let me continue. You are strong, you are powerful, and you never cease to impress me. I think I loved you before I even knew or admitted it to myself. I feel like I've been searching for you my entire life. Like I've loved you since before I met you."

Her eyes glisten as she remains quiet, her lips slightly parting. "Why are you telling me this?"

I reach for the button of her jeans, popping it slowly. "Because, I've wanted you to know for some time now. And because I plan on proving my love to you in every way imaginable, and after I do this, you are going to be mine forever, just as I am going to be yours."

She mashes her lips against mine once more, eagerly and I don't even have to hear her say it back. I know she wants me just as badly as I want her. I know she loves me just as deeply as I love her. I slip the jeans down her legs as she quivers from my touch, then I pick her up and lay her down on the bed, before crawling on top of her.

Her fingers graze the bare skin of my chest, leaving a path of tingles in its wake. It's amazing how such a small gesture can rile me up so quickly.

As I begin to trail my kisses and my tongue over her sinfully sweet skin, I realize that she is the one who saved me from the darkness. She gave me a reason to fight, to continue on. We may have had a rocky start, but there is no one else in the world that has ever made my bones hum the way she does. The world has a long way to go before it's back to being normal, but Phoenix is my world, she is my reason for living.

As I slip inside of her, I know that we can face anything, as long as we are together.

*   *   *

A frenzied pounding jolts me awake. My hand immediately drops down to the bed, reaching out for Phoenix, but her side of the bed is empty. My heart begins racing as the pounding only increases. I quickly throw on my underwear and tug on my pants, not bothering to zip them up as I rush to open the door. A wide-eyed Ike is staring back at me. "Is she in here?" he asks, frantically, poking his head around me and into the room.

I shake my head. "Have you checked her room?"

He is shaking as he nods. "They're gone."

"What?" I ask, my heart beating against my chest.

"They're all gone."

I peek my head out into the hallway nervously. "What are you talking about, Ike?"

"The President. His staff. Cruz. Phoenix. Jean-Luc. They're gone."

Preview of a new fantasy novel by Kira Adams, *Reality Squared*:

One
The Beginning

Sahara Rose

I never imagined such cold, heartless, hatred, but after the city lost power, it was every man for himself; Droma against Droma. Kill or be killed. Two sides emerged early on in the war for survival. One was all about power. The other was all about family, survival, and hope. Good Droma's vs. bad Droma's. Unfortunately for us, the bloodthirsty bastards had the upper hand. They had the resources, they had the man power. Join them or be killed, simple as that; they were starting a revolution.

It was three years into the war, and nearly half of our planet had been wiped out by its devastation. I had been on the run for so long, I didn't remember what a real meal tasted like, what a real bed felt like. I had been lucky enough to align myself with a few other good Droma's I found along the way.

I had been with Mae Porter the longest. She was the most amazingly beautiful Korean, with jet black straight hair that surpassed her rear, hazel eyes, and the rosiest of cheeks. We had come upon each other while squatting in abandoned properties, attempting to stay alive. I knew right away I could trust her because the other side, the ones who went by "The Immorals", had a mark. It was something that could not be hidden as they made sure to put it in plain sight—right on the face, to the right of the eye, they were all left with scars that appeared to resemble tears; small enough they could get within a close enough range to harm us, but important enough to them, because they lived by a motto: no Droma left behind. They also had terrible repercussions if one of their own turned on them; I had heard one too many horror stories.

Mae had also come to be one of my biggest assets in the war, as she could freeze time and choose the elements that were affected in the room for up to fifteen minutes. I had come to trust her with my life. I had been with her long enough, and she had never crossed me. She was the closest thing that I could call family.

We met Zeke Forrester a year ago. He was this incredibly handsome blond haired, blue eyed, ripped, tan, GOD. I was positive he had been implanted from another planet because of his intense beauty. It was so out of place. He seemed so unfazed. I was beginning to wonder if he took swings for the same team. But then again, maybe he was just quiet. In the time he had been with us, he had said a total of twenty things. It seemed as though he saved his words for when they were needed most. I had this strange déjà vu feeling whenever he did speak. I just didn't know what to think of him. He was so mysterious. I had come to learn his asset to this war was extreme hearing. Zeke's incredible hearing had saved our lives more times than I could count, so I made the decision to trust him.

Lastly, six months ago, we picked up Fallon Edwards, a fiery red head with a pixie cut and more freckles than I could count. Eyes as blue as the ocean, tiny, petite, and barely breaking 5'0". She was so tiny and fragile when we picked her up, we were all unconsciously looking out for her. It was strange; it was almost like I felt it was something I *had* to do, not something that I *wanted* to do, but I felt like I had no choice. Now I realize I was entranced by her. That's right; she could make anyone do anything with just the bat of an eye. I never felt safe with her, I never felt like I could trust her fully, but we were lacking in numbers, and what she brought to the table was impressive.

Even though we knew our side was completely

outnumbered, it still felt nice to have closeness like a family. It made us passionate. It made us better fighters. I also knew we were in for the fight for our lives, and had been given a vision of the future from a fellow Droma we met along the way. It was a vision of me fighting alongside a brown-haired, green-eyed, generic looking female, but when she grabbed my hand, I was overcome with emotion and familiarity. I was not scared. I knew she was going to win this war for us. The connection was undeniable. She was another version of me; a better version of me. The most I knew was that she was living in an alternate reality. I had been searching for a way to travel between the realities since I was given the vision, but had been unsuccessful.

Mae, Zeke, Fallon, and I were holed up in an abandoned mansion I had been scouting for weeks. Today was the first day I felt comfortable enough to let my group even enter the premises. We decided to make camp there, out of the rain.

"Sahara." Mae waved me over, "I think I just hit the jackpot." She grinned, ear to ear, scooping up as many cans of food as her tiny arms could carry.

"Don't get too excited, have you made sure they're not booby-trapped?" I raised my eyebrows, cautiously.

"Yes ma'am," Mae joked, "I did everything you have taught me. Now can we eat?"

We had been sharing nothing more than a few cans of food a day between the four of us. To find an abandoned building with a modular packed full, seemed too out of the ordinary. I knew she had said she'd checked, but it still felt like a trap to me. "Go ahead," I exclaimed wary, heading towards the stairs.

"Where ya going?" Zeke called after me.

"Someone's gotta keep watch, right?" I replied, without looking back. I headed for the front door; it seemed like the only logical thing. I climbed down the enormous spiral staircase, and plopped myself at the base of it, gripping my machete tight.

Seconds turned to minutes. Minutes shifted to hours. And try as hard as I might, I couldn't fight the fatigue any longer. Without really thinking straight, I closed my eyes slowly, my head falling against the marble wall.

*   *   *

"Ouch," I groaned, gently rubbing the right side of my head. It felt like a ton of bricks had fallen on it. Slowly, I lifted my eyelids open, but the sight I came to see, was far from expected. I was staring down the barrel of an ancient Colt M1911. I couldn't remember the last time I had seen a gun, or found excess bullets. The other side had wiped the planet clean of them. But something drew my attention away; something slowed my heart beat. I knew the stranger had felt it too, when he suddenly lowered the gun.

I wasn't sure how long my mouth had been hanging wide open, but I closed it, embarrassedly, before assessing just what I was looking at. I had read about it in my books of fairytales when I was a little girl, I had even heard stories as I grew older, but I had never in a million years thought I would be staring at *this*.

The Droma staring back at me had a magenta light that outlined his entire shape. In the fairytales it was written that true love was always highlighted. That no matter where you were or *who* you were, if you ever came across them, you would instantly know because of the light surrounding them; it was something only the two soul mates could see. It was also rumored that the light had a calming effect on the "soul mate". I was beginning to understand this first hand.

My eyes trailed his frame from top to bottom,

taking ample time to savor every moment. He was probably no taller than 5'8", but he had short chocolate colored hair, the most astonishing sapphire eyes, and muscles everywhere. They were bulging out of his too small tank. He was covered in tattoos, he had sleeves of them, and I was curious if there was a bare inch of his skin that wasn't covered in tattoos.

Our eyes crossed paths, and I realized he had been taking the very same opportunity soaking me in. I blushed a little, wondering what he thought of my dirty old clothes, and unruly black curls. "Is this really happening?" he asked me in disbelief.

I nodded my head lightly, still unable to process a clear thought.

"My mother used to tell me bedtime stories as a young lad," he drawled in what I could only assume was an Irish accent. "I just never believed it could hold any validity." He was still staring so intently on me, it was making me uncomfortable.

I stood up from the stairs, turning away from him. "How do you have a gun?" I whispered over my shoulder.

I felt him take a step towards me, and it's like I

lost control. I lost control of everything. I couldn't think right, I couldn't see straight. All I could feel was his warm breath on the back of my neck, sending goose bumps all over my body.

I was trembling, and I was sure he was aware of it. I felt my hair being swept to my right shoulder, and then it was like magic. The instant his fingers brushed barely against my skin; I felt it. It was an overwhelming feeling of love, comfort, knowing. I was seeing a slideshow in my head of different couples, all over the world, different realities, different times, different planets, but I *knew* them. They were us. The fairytales were right. I had met this man over and over again in different lives and different times, but we had always found each other; and were destined to.

I felt like my heart was bursting with love. The stranger he had been to me less than ten minutes ago had all but disappeared. Even though his face was new to me, his body, his accent….this was someone I had known longer than anyone else in my entire life. This was someone I had been secretly searching for since I was a little girl, and dreamed of falling in love with. He had been who I had been praying for to help us in our fight against the *Immorals*. And yet, I didn't even know his name…all I knew was that I running out of time.

I spun around suddenly not worried about an answer to my question. "How am I going to be able to explain you?" I asked quietly, more to myself than anything else, before snatching my machete from the stairs and whacking him with the handle, knocking him out cold, sending him crashing to the floor loudly.

Acknowledgements

Thank you to my entire street team for the enthusiasm you showed for this book. If it wasn't for you guys, I'm not sure I would have released Emerging from Darkness so quickly. You guys reminded me how much I love the characters and their individual voices; you brought back the passion I felt when I wrote the first book. It is because of your feedback and help that Emerging from Darkness is as strong as it is today. So thank you my believers for doing what you do best, believing in my characters, their stories, and me.

Thank you Melissa, Tina, Krystal, and Sara for always jumping at the chance to help me out whenever I need a second opinion or simply an ear to vent to. You guys are such a big reason why I continue to follow my dreams. Thank you so much for everything you have done, will do, and continue to do for me. I appreciate it more than you will ever know.

Don't forget—if you're not doing something you love, you're not really living.

Kira Adams

About the author:

Krista Pakseresht has always been a dreamer. From the first time she opened her eyes. Creating worlds through words is one thing she is truly talented at. She specializes in Young adult/New adult romance, horror, action, fantasy, and non-fiction under the pen name [Kira Adams](). She is the author of the [Infinite Love series](), the [Foundation series](), the Darkness Falls series, and the Looking Glass series.

Want to stay up to date with all the new releases, cover reveals, never-before-seen-excerpts, and more? Sign up for the Kira Adams newsletter [here]().

Books by Kira Adams:

The Infinite Love Series
Learning to Live (Ciera & Topher)
My Forever (Madalynne & Parker)
Beautifully Broken (Jacqueline & Lee)
Against All Odds (Austyn & Avery)

The Foundation Series
Pieces of Me
The Fighter

Darkness Falls Series
Into the Darkness
Emerging from Darkness

Made in the USA
San Bernardino, CA
20 April 2015